SLIVERING CURSE

THE QUEEN'S FAYTE
BOOK TWO

THE QUEEN'S FAYTE SERIES

SLIVERING CURSE

THE QUEEN'S FAYTE
BOOK TWO

D.D. CROIX

Fine Skylark Media
California

Fine Skylark Media
P.O. Box 1505
Lake Forest, California 92609-1505

Cover provided by Karri Klawiter
Editing services provided by Katrina Roets

D.D Croix
Slivering Curse: The Queen's Fayte Book Two:
by D.D. Croix — 1st ed.
[1. Teen and Young Adult, Science Fiction and Fantasy,
Historical — Fiction. 2. Teen and Young Adult, Mysteries
and Thrillers, Fantasy and Supernatural — Fiction. 3.
Science Fiction and Fantasy, Fantasy, Coming of Age —
Fiction. 4. Science Fiction and Fantasy, Fantasy, Dark
Fantasy — Fiction. 5. Science Fiction and Fantasy, Fantasy,
Myths and Legends — Fiction.]

DEDICATION

For Diane

CHAPTER ONE

FORGET THE FEAR. *Forget the doubt.*

I shoved back my sleeves and squared myself to my adversary. I'd saved Queen Victoria from a monster and nearly met my own demise for goodness' sake. I wouldn't be defeated by a porridge.

The lid rattled atop the copper pot as I paced beside the stove and gnawed my lower lip. Had I set the flame too high or allowed too much steam to escape? Mentally, I ran through the checklist of steps, then I did it again.

Finally, the cook overseeing my work in the Balmoral Castle kitchen gave me the nod, and I lifted the pot's top to peer inside.

Was it possible? Did I dare to hope? It had taken the better part of an hour, but the bubbling semolina porridge had reduced to an edible consistency, not too soupy and not a scorched ruin like every other attempt.

I pulled away the cover. "It looks ready. Do you agree, Miss Bellington?"

She left her bowl of freshly sifted flour to glance over my shoulder. "I wish you would call me Clara. We're not so fussy here, not like Windsor." She pulled back and touched her lips. "I don't mean *you're* fussy. I mean

1

everyone else. No, what I mean is—"

I waved off her flustered apology. "It's all right. I know what you mean." I turned back to the porridge so she wouldn't see me suck in my cheeks to hide a smile. It wasn't that I enjoyed her embarrassment, but I still wasn't used to being someone who could fluster others, especially someone like Clara Bellington. She was only a few years older than I was, yet she'd already established herself as a cook in the royal kitchen. Granted, it was usually the morning cook for the serving staff, which numbered less than half that at Windsor, but she was a full-fledged cook, nonetheless.

One day I hoped to follow in those footsteps, although at the moment, I'd be happy to produce a decent porridge. After all, that's why I was here: to help while the castle's House Steward searched for a junior cook to fill a vacancy.

At least that was the official reason for my visit.

The true purpose had more to do with my recent initiation into the Order of the Fayte, an ancient society of royal guardians that has kept its existence secret for centuries by operating as ordinary castle servants while discreetly protecting Britain's kings and queens. They manage it with the help of Druansha, an ethereal woman they call the Lady of the Fayte who, like the legendary fae, possesses mysterious talents and an ability to move between worlds.

Druansha can sometimes warn Fayte Guardians about potential threats to Her Majesty Queen Victoria, yet she herself had the misfortune of being trapped in dragonfly form for several years before I broke the curse her malicious brother had placed on her. Releasing her not only restored her as the Fayte Guardians' oracle but prevented that brute from taking control of our Queen and her empire.

In appreciation for my efforts, the Order arranged to send me here, along with my friend Marlie for moral support, so I might search the Fayte records for information about my parents and how I came to be placed at Chadwick Hollow School for Orphaned Girls as a child. Since I have no memory of anything prior to my arrival at that institution, I have relied on the word of my mentor, Mrs. Crossey, that my ability to see visions means Fayte Guardian blood flows through me and that the answers to my forgotten past might be found here in the Scottish Highlands.

I might have passed on the opportunity if we hadn't been joined on our journey by Lucas Starwyck, an enigmatic young man who'd kept his true identity a mystery until just a few weeks ago because he'd been charged with the clandestine task of protecting the Queen from me because certain Fayte Guardians believed I was a danger to her.

In the end, he proved himself an ally and true friend. Until we reached Balmoral a week ago, I thought he might be more than that, but since we'd arrived, he's made himself so scarce, I no longer know what to think.

Right now, however, this confounded porridge required all of my attention.

Clara lowered her wooden spoon into the pot and stirred. Her lips pinched in disapproval. "It's nearly there. We still need to work on the clumping. Now let's see about the taste." She grabbed a clean teaspoon and dabbed it in the mixture. After a nibble, she tried to smile but coughed instead. "A bit too much salt, but otherwise it's coming along. It's definitely coming along. Let's try it one more time, then we'll call it a day."

I bit back my disappointment.

She glanced around, lowered her voice, and lifted a single eyebrow. "Tomorrow is *you know what,* but I could take you tonight, so you can have a look around."

I pasted a smile on my face. "Thank you. I'd like that." I turned back to my failed porridge before letting the false cheer slip away. Anyone who overheard us might assume she was referring to the castle, but I'd already seen plenty of that. We both knew she meant Balmoral's Fayte Hall, which contained the archives I was sent to see.

Since my arrival, Clara was my only official connection to the local Order and would remain so until tomorrow's New Moon, the time when Fayte Guardians gather for a Converging Ceremony to communicate with Druansha. Although Clara had already offered several times to escort me to the hall, I'd managed to make excuses each time.

My disinterest probably confused her, but my past no longer consumed me, especially not after the warm welcome I'd received here at Balmoral. Little more than a week had passed, but I was thinking more clearly now than I had after the Windsor ordeal, and I was no longer desperate for the validation I'd hoped to find in the archives.

I'd been drawn in by the claim made by Druansha's brother, that horrible gargoyle of a man who called himself Krol, but now I saw the truth. He couldn't be my father. It had been a desperate attempt to prey on my weakness, that was all. To be honest, I was embarrassed to have fallen for it, even for a moment.

So, I was in no hurry to visit their Fayte Hall, but I didn't mind being excused from the kitchen early. For the first time in my life, I was eager to get to the Servants' Hall to chat and laugh with colleagues over the day's events. If it meant I might also cross paths with Lucas Starwyck, I wouldn't mind that, either.

When Clara returned to sifting her flour, I grabbed a fresh teaspoon and tasted the porridge myself. My lips curled, and I struggled to swallow the clumpy mess. Her assessment had been too kind. The stuff was awful.

Grabbing the pot by both handles, I carried it to the buckets where we collected scraps that could be fed to the livestock. After I'd dumped it, I used a rag to wipe the splatter from my new lambskin gloves, a gift from Mrs. Crossey to replace the ones I'd damaged while helping Druansha back at Windsor. I was doing my best to keep this pair clean, though I hoped the Faytling crystal tucked snugly beneath my collar would eventually help me control my visions so I wouldn't need the gloves at all.

Until then, even casual contact with someone could send me hurtling into a vision of their past—and if I focused and if I was lucky, their present and future as well. So, the gloves remained necessary. At least no one had questioned why I never took them off, though I suspected Mrs. Crossey had something to do with that as well.

When I returned to our worktable, Clara had a visitor. A maid in a starched and ruffled pinafore stood beside her.

"Why haven't you gone?" Clara said in a hurried whisper, her shoulders rigid and tense.

"I've been busy," the other whispered back. "But I will."

"Soon?"

They were trying not to be overheard, so I turned my back and pretended to be engrossed in a row of hanging copper pots and pans.

The other young woman hissed, "Yes, soon. If you're so anxious, we can go tonight."

Clara huffed. "I have plans tonight."

"Then don't say I didn't offer."

Clara made a grumbling sound in the back of her throat. "Fine, we'll go tonight. But I need a few minutes."

"Better hurry. I want to be back before dark."

I turned to watch the parlor maid walk away. She stopped when she saw me.

"Hello," I said. "I'm Jane."

For the past week, I'd met one friendly colleague after another. Strangers turned up out of the blue to introduce themselves, and those who didn't always brightened when I told them I was visiting from Windsor.

This young woman didn't brighten at all. Her face flashed surprise, then her nose crinkled as she passed me without a word.

Clara caught the exchange and fidgeted like she'd been caught doing something she shouldn't. "You're back, good. About tonight, I'm afraid something has come up."

"Don't worry. We can go another time." The words were quicker and more enthusiastic than I'd intended, and it didn't go unnoticed.

I glanced back to where the prickly maid had disappeared. "Who was that?" It was an obvious attempt to change the subject, but it still seemed like a valid question.

"I'm sorry. I should have introduced you. That's my sister, Ada."

"Your sister?" I looked more closely at the young woman striding toward the corridor. She was taller than Clara but just as slender and her hair was the same ash brown shade, though smoother than Clara's tightly wound curls. I suppose there was a family resemblance.

"I tried to introduce myself, but she was in a hurry." I could see on Clara's face she'd seen what really happened.

"I'm sorry about that. She can be a bit…"

"Tense?"

She grinned. "Yes, that's one way to put it."

"Anything I can do to help?"

"No but thank you." She glanced around and lowered her voice. "I really am sorry about… you know." She flashed puppy dog eyes.

I feigned disappointment. "I completely understand, and I'll see it tomorrow anyway."

"We'll go early," she continued, "so you can have a good look around before things get started."

"I'll look forward to it." And I would, too. Although I didn't care about the old records anymore, I was eager to attend the ceremony. I hadn't seen Druansha since my initiation, and even though she was no longer the dragonfly who'd been my companion for so long, it would be good to see her again.

And, of course, Lucas would be there.

"I can finish things here," she said. "You may as well…" Her gaze drifted back to the door. "Isn't that your friend?"

I turned to see Marlie entering the kitchen on her way to Servants' Hall. I still hardly recognized her in the ruffled apron and lacy bonnet. Since we'd arrived, she'd been assigned to the sitting rooms, where she mainly dusted furniture and tended the potted plants since the royal family wasn't in residence. It was a significant step up from scullery maid, but I sensed she would have preferred to remain in the kitchen. She waved when she saw me.

"She must be on her meal break. Would it be all right if I joined her?"

Clara was already removing her apron. "Of course. I'll see you tomorrow."

"Bright and early." I tugged off my own apron and left it on a hook beside the worktable before setting off toward Marlie, maneuvering around the other cooks and maids who were preparing the evening meal for the household, which constituted a few royal relations and a dignitary from Brussels who had come on business weeks ago and seemed in no hurry to leave.

"Off so early? How'd you manage that?" Marlie asked when I approached.

Her long, honey-colored hair was twisted back in a bun beneath her white bonnet, and her freckles seemed to dance across her nose.

"I'd like to think it was a reward for a job well done, but the truth is, Miss Bellington was called away."

"Really? By whom?"

We pushed through the swinging door to the Servants' Hall to find small clusters of maids, footmen, and other servants huddled along the long table. Each was already chin deep in stew and daily chatter. We grabbed bowls and filled them from the pot set upon the sideboard alongside a basket of biscuits still warm from the oven.

"She said it was her sister. An upstairs maid named Ada. Have you met her?"

I took my bowl and slipped into an empty chair beside four young maids who motioned for us to join them.

The one closest to me, a striking figure with pale yellow hair, leaned close and whispered, "Are you referring to Ada Bellington?"

I plunged my spoon into my bowl and chased a carrot slice, wondering if I'd said something I shouldn't. "Do you know her?"

My neighbor exchanged weighty looks with the others in her group then dropped her chin and whispered, "She's a bit…"

"Too big for her knickers?" another beside her offered, sending the others into a fit of giggles.

I held a straight face. "I'm afraid I may have offended her. When I tried to introduce myself, she rushed away like her tail was on fire."

A third young woman with a more serious demeanor piped in. "Don't take it personally. The poor girl's probably just missing her mum."

The others muttered agreement, and the one closest to me cleared her throat. "Where are my manners? I should have introduced myself. I'm Ivy. I work up in the guest apartments. We all do." She pointed to her neighbor. "Dinah." Her finger moved to the serious lass across from her. "Dove, and that's Deirdre."

Both young women across the table waved.

"You two are from Windsor, right?" she asked.

"We are." I introduced Marlie and myself and explained that Marlie was working in the sitting rooms during our stay.

When Marlie said hello, Ivy leaned toward her. "Is that the Highlands I hear in your voice?"

"Aye." Marlie turned a bright pink. "But my family moved to Windsor when I was still a wee bairn."

Marlie had never referred to a "wee" anything before. All the Scottish air must be stirring up old memories.

"Pity," Ivy replied then turned to me. "Are you from this side of the Borders?"

"I can't say that I am." I looked away and hoped that was the end of her questions.

Of course, I was never that lucky.

"You're in the kitchen, aren't you?" she pressed.

"I am."

She spun back to Dinah. "See? I told you." Then she turned back to me. "Maybe you can settle an argument. I heard the night cook ate an entire lamb shank during his shift, and when he was caught, he tried to blame it on the dogs. Dinah heard the same story, except that he blamed a band of village boys who had sneaked in when the guards weren't looking. Which one is true?"

I wasn't surprised the story had spread. Everyone within earshot of the kitchen that morning had heard the chef screaming at the cook who had been in charge of roasting three lamb shanks overnight because a good portion of one of them was missing. The young man claimed he'd turned away to check on a stockpot, and when he turned back, the chunk was gone.

"He blamed dogs," I said, "but the chef didn't believe him because the leg had obviously been cut with a knife, not ripped by teeth."

"I told you." Ivy jostled Dinah, who seemed to take the loss in stride. After more laughter, she turned to me. "You keep staring at the door. Why?"

"Don't mind her," Marlie answered before I could. "She's waiting for someone."

"Oh?" the chambermaids said nearly in unison. Goofy

9

grins spread across their faces like they'd caught me with a juicy secret.

Ordinarily, I would have bristled at that kind of attention, but not anymore. Everything was different at Balmoral. For the first time in my life, I had friends. I had a purpose. And maybe, if I could trust these unfamiliar feelings that kept my gaze locked on that door, I might even have something more.

"Is it someone special?" Ivy pressed.

I tried to hold back my ridiculous grin, but it didn't work. "Yes, he is. He's quite special."

"What's his name?"

Marlie flashed me a look, and I knew what she was thinking. Would I be honest—with these new friends and myself? Or, would I keep denying what she's known since Windsor?

"Lucas," I said. "His name's Lucas Starwyck. You must know him." The way their eyes darted away and they fidgeted with their food told me they did.

Only Ivy looked back at me. She gave me the weakest of smiles. "Of course. Everyone knows Lucas. He's wonderful, isn't he? Such a charmer and always full of surprises." She glanced at the clock. "Oh, is it so late already? I should be getting back."

She didn't say where she needed to go, only grabbed her dishes and made for the door. Her friends followed behind with hasty goodbyes.

Marlie stared at their backs, looking puzzled. "What do you suppose that was about?"

I shook my head, but the thumping in my chest told me it couldn't be good.

CHAPTER TWO

A CLOCK IN a distant room struck its eleventh chime as Marlie and I approached the butler's pantry.

"Clara said to wait for her here," I whispered, hoping I wouldn't be overheard by anyone lingering in the kitchen. It didn't seem likely, however. Even in the dim glow of the single night lantern, the place appeared to be deserted.

"How long should we wait?" Marlie's glance chased the shadows flickering across the walls.

"Not long," said a cheerful voice from beneath an ominously black hood. The cloaked figure emerged from the dark corridor like a wraith, but I knew in an instant it was Clara.

She motioned us toward the door. "Hurry, get inside before we're seen." She pulled it closed without a sound, which left us in utter darkness until she struck a match.

I'd visited this pantry so many times over the past week without ever suspecting it held a portal to Balmoral's Fayte Hall. Now, because of the candlelight or maybe the awareness of the secret, it looked different. It *felt* different. The tiny orange flame reflected off the long rows of whitewashed cabinets, and I wondered how many more secrets it might hold.

"This way." Clara had moved to the end of the narrow room, where she cupped the underside of a shelf with one hand as she held the candle with the other. There was a low groan and the click of a hinge, then with surprising ease, she pulled a length of the cabinet away from the wall, revealing an opening.

"C'mon." Clara gestured for Marlie and me to enter.

I followed, with Marlie on my heels.

The space inside was tight, and once the cabinet was again flush with the wall, Clara took the lead as we descended a straight stone staircase.

I counted thirty-four steps before we reached the bottom, which opened to what looked like the edge of a cavernous hall. I squinted into the blackness, trying to see beyond the candle's glow.

"Are you all right?" Clara asked, no longer whispering.

I hesitated, taking in the smooth stone walls and polished flagstone floor. The craftsmanship was exquisite. "Your hall is beautiful."

"Oh, this isn't the hall," she replied, amused. "Not yet. We have to get through the tunnel first."

"*This* is the tunnel?" Marlie gaped at the arched ceiling and the elegant niches set into the walls like picture frames, each containing an ornamental bronze bowl atop a pedestal.

I was surprised, too. Windsor Castle's tunnel was dusty and old and smelled of rat droppings. "This is so clean." I took a deep breath. "The air smells fresh."

"You should have seen it when it was new," Clara said. "It was built before the replacement castle, so it's gotten a bit shabby over the years. It could use a proper cleaning."

It had been little more than a decade since the royal family purchased the land with its 16th century castle and commissioned a larger, more suitable castle soon after. Work began on the new structure almost immediately but had been completed only a few years before.

Still, Clara ran a finger over the ledge of the nearest niche, looked at it, and shook her head. "It definitely needs some attention. But watch this." She extended her candle toward the bowl in the niche, and in an instant, a gust of flame filled the vessel, lighting the room and revealing that it was, indeed, the beginning of a tunnel.

"That's clever." I poked my head into the niche to see what fueled the fire, but the heat kept me from getting too close.

Clara lifted her finger, signaling us to wait then pointed deeper into the darkness. A heartbeat later, a new flame ignited in the next niche, then another after that, and another until bowls were aflame as far as we could see.

"How did you do that?" I mused.

"It's something the builders dreamed up. That panel there"—she gestured to a brass plate on the wall beneath the niche—"is a switch that will extinguish them all as well. If no movement is detected out here after a few moments, they go out on their own. It's quite convenient." She blew softly on her candle's flame to put it out.

As we followed Clara, I questioned whether this could even be called a tunnel. It seemed more like an exhaustively long corridor with no doors, only an occasional elegant chair or cabinet set against the wall, creating the illusion that we were in a well-appointed home not a subterranean passageway.

When the end came into view, I could finally see the door.

"That's the entrance to your hall?" I regretted my disapproving tone, but the portal to Windsor Castle's Fayte Hall was nearly two stories tall and flanked by towering stone pillars. This one, I wasn't even sure it was a door. I saw no handle, only something like a decorative relief of a yawning dragon at its center.

"You'll see. Here, hold this." Clara handed me her brass candleholder and fidgeted with her collar.

"What kind of door has no knob?" Marlie whispered, voicing my own question.

"Be patient." Clara released her Faytling from beneath her blouse. "Our Faytlings act like keys." She lifted the crystal amulet from around her neck and touched it to the dragon's open mouth. She tapped the Faytling gently until it notched into place. Immediately, the crystal began to glow.

Something deep in the wall clanked, and the door slid open.

My hand fluttered to my own Faytling hidden beneath my blouse.

"How did you do that?" Marlie leaned close to the edge of the frame, looking for the place where the lock had engaged and released.

"It has something to do with the Lady's crystals, that's all I know. Any Faytling can unlock it. You can probably get a better explanation from Mr. Starwyck or his son since they designed it."

"They did?" I ran a finger over the contours of the relief.

"Why do you sound surprised?" Clara was almost laughing. "The Starwycks oversaw the construction of everything down here, with the Fayte Council's guidance, of course."

"Truly? He never mentioned it." I pulled back my hand. Perhaps at Windsor there hadn't been an opportunity, but along the journey north? Two weeks in a carriage and all those quiet nights in front of the fires at the cozy inns where we'd stopped. We'd discussed so many things, private things I'd never shared with another soul, not even Marlie. I thought he'd been sharing with me as well, but how could he not have mentioned this? Perhaps he hadn't been as candid as I'd thought.

Clara returned her Faytling to her neck, leaving the crystal on top of her blouse instead of hiding it beneath, then motioned us inside. "Here we are. Welcome to Balmoral's Fayte Hall."

~ ~ ~

Like the tunnel, the hall's interior wasn't at all what I expected. Windsor Castle's Fayte Hall could have been the remains of a medieval stone keep, but this place was as refined as any royal sitting room. Polished mahogany paneled the walls, vibrant rugs covered the floor, and collegiate chairs and tables had been arranged around the room, creating a space that was equally studious and elegant, with gas lamps along the wall that were already alight.

"Is someone here?" I asked. Surely the lights didn't light themselves.

Clara shook her head. "The same mechanism that triggers the tunnel's lamps triggers these as well. Convenient, don't you think?"

"Quite," Marlie and I said in unison.

"But where are the books?" Marlie added, her gaze roaming the walls.

She was right. I searched for shelves but saw only a towering grandfather clock and a handful of glass cabinets filled with curious items. The nearest one held a shiny silver chalice with a golden band studded with rose-colored crystals sitting beside a cloak pin and a dagger with a jeweled hilt. When I moved closer, I saw a brass plaque on it that read *Artifacts of Boudica, Queen of Britannia and first Fayte Guardian.* Another cabinet along the left wall held a thick tome covered in aged leather engraved with *The Scryer Record* in flourishing script. This place looked more like a museum than a library.

"The books are up there," Clara pointed upward, and my gaze followed.

I squinted, trying to see, but the gas lamps installed

along the walls were too dim to help. Clara reached for a velvet bell pull beside the door, and when she tugged it, the lamps brightened, and the fire that had been smoldering low in the hearth roared to life. I marveled at so many lamps set along the walls above until I realized many of them were merely reflections in mirrors. Another clever innovation, to be sure.

In the amplified light, I could see the coffered ceiling soared thirty, maybe forty feet over our heads and two more floors ringed the room's central pillars like indoor balconies.

I stumbled and nearly lost my balance as I gazed upward. "It's so grand." My words were breathless and entirely inadequate, but it was all I could manage.

Clara hardly noticed as she reached into a wardrobe and pulled out indigo robes. Finally, something that reminded me of Windsor. The robes were exactly the same, even down to the small metal fastener at the collar and the wide bell sleeves. She handed one to Marlie and another to me.

Marlie tugged hers over her shoulders and smoothed the front. "Are we the first to arrive, then?"

"The others will be along soon," Clara said. "I wanted you to have a look around before the place fills up. Come on."

She led us to a black wrought-iron staircase that ascended like a corkscrew to the upper levels. When we reached the second landing, I saw the space was wider than it appeared from below, with upholstered chairs and side tables outfitted with reading lamps.

I frowned. "I still don't see any books."

Clara's eyes twinkled. "They're in here. Look." She approached a small brass square set into the middle of a mahogany panel. Sharply etched letters spelled out Balmoral I. She glanced over her shoulder at Marlie and me. "You'll want to step back."

When we did, she touched the plaque. Something behind the wall clicked, and the panel sprang away from the wall. She grabbed an edge and pulled out an entirely hidden bookcase. Fully extended, the rolling shelf, with three long rows of identical black volumes, must have been eight feet long. The earthy smell of all those leather covers tickled my nose.

"These are mostly employment records, house accounts, reports on best practices, and miscellaneous instructions compiled through the years. If you tell me what you're looking for, I can probably help you find it."

Marlie watched me with interest. Although both of them had been told I was here to learn about the Order since I was so new to it, I knew Marlie suspected there was more to it. She didn't know I had no memory of my childhood and was searching for clues about my parents, however. Only Mrs. Crossey knew that, and I had no intention of bringing anyone else in on the secret.

I did my best to shrug off Clara's remark. "I'm not looking for anything in particular. Just trying to learn what I can."

Marlie's glance drifted from me to the bookshelf. She grabbed a volume and opened it. "Look at this. Notes on cleaning old weapons and armor. It's even illustrated."

She tilted the book so I could see the flourishing script next to an excellent sketch of a longsword.

"To remove rust from the metal surface," she read, "immerse in petroleum oil for more than two but not more than four hours, then rub gently with a soft cloth. Repeat, as necessary."

"We have a little bit of everything," Clara said with a chuckle. "Information on every assignment, every task, everything that might help the castle run smoothly, along with a proper accounting of all the comings and goings, and everyone's position in the Order."

Marlie went to the next wall panel and brushed her

fingers over it. "Is this another shelf?"

Clara glided the first shelf back into the wall. "That one contains the family collections."

Marlie pushed the panel's plaque, engraved with Balmoral II, just as Clara had, and another rolling shelf popped out, revealing more rows of identical black leather books.

Clara ran her fingers along the middle row. "This is where we record the Balmoral Fayte families' births and deaths, the weddings and promotions. An accounting of all the important events that happen in our lives, just as the other regions do." She removed a volume and opened it, flipping pages until she stopped at one. "This is my mother's last entry. *Lavinia Bellington, retired from service as First Scryer and second chamber mistress on the Seventh of April, Eighteen Fifty-Nine.* I think inscribing this was one of the last things she did before she left."

Her wistful look said more than any words could about how much she missed her mother. I was about to ask where the elder Bellington had gone when Marlie interrupted.

"This can't be all of it, though." Marlie was examining the walls, searching for additional panels.

"What do you mean?" Clara returned her family's volume to the shelf.

"Everything that came from Windsor. We had dozens of old journals and scrolls from the old days. They were sent here for safekeeping. Where are they?"

"You mean those silly old magic books?"

I don't think Clara meant to hurt Marlie's feelings, but I could see the pain in my friend's expression.

"Yes, I suppose I do mean those old magic books," Marlie said, and I knew she was straining to be polite. We were still guests, after all. "You do have them, don't you?"

"Of course. We never get rid of anything. They're probably up there." She pointed to the level above us.

"That's also where you'll find the oldest logs and everything we inherited from Windsor, Buckingham, and the others. I'm not sure what you're looking for, but whatever it is, I should probably warn you that no one's been up there since Mrs. Travers left."

"Who's Mrs. Travers?" I asked.

"She was the archivist the Council put in charge of organizing everything up there. She was not only glacially slow, she was also one of the first maids to be let go when the efficiency dismissals began."

The efficiency dismissals, as they were called, had started several months before when Prince Albert decided the royal household was overstaffed. He initiated a campaign to reduce the ranks, but what he didn't know was the redundancy had masked the secret work of a legion of Fayte Guardians. By dismissing them, he removed a number of those who protected the Queen and her family from threats they never even knew existed.

The loss had not only compromised the Order's ability to protect the Queen to a near-fatal degree but also prompted a few resentful Guardians to concoct a threat meant to force Prince Albert to reverse course. Unfortunately, the plot's author, a Fayte High Councilor named Edward Bailey, succumbed to Krol's promises of power, and the man would have allowed that monster to take possession of Queen Victoria herself if we hadn't stopped him.

After that fiasco, the Queen ended the dismissals, and many of the lost Guardians were hired back. But not all of them, and apparently not this one.

"Why did they move the old records and collections here?" I asked. "Wouldn't it have been safer to leave them where they were?"

"It was mostly a matter of preservation," Clara said. "Some of the older texts were deteriorating and starting to show their age. Mold and mites in the Windsor Library were wreaking havoc on the oldest texts, and Buckingham wasn't much better. This place, however, was built to provide a better, safer environment."

Marlie's fingertips brushed the wood paneling. "It's certainly cleaner. No dust, no musty smells."

"That's only part of it." Clara tilted her head. "Do you hear that buzzing?"

I listened and noticed a churning, almost grinding sound coming from behind the wall. "What is it?"

She pointed at a vented brass plate in the paneling below the first balcony. "There's a machine behind there that regulates the temperature and humidity in here. It makes adjustments if the levels move beyond certain parameters."

I'd heard of machines doing incredible things, but altering the air? What sort of machine could do that? "Can we see it?"

She shook her head. "The only people allowed back there are the operators."

That only heightened my curiosity. "Who are the operators?"

She crinkled her nose as though my question surprised her. "The Starwycks, of course."

"Lucas?" I asked.

She nodded.

I could hardly believe it. How many secrets had he kept from me?

Clara shifted and glanced back toward the machine's hiding place. "You know, I've only seen it once myself, and it really is quite a wonder. Since you're honored guests and all, maybe it wouldn't hurt to bend the rule just a wee bit. Would you really like to see it?"

I bit back a smile. I did want to see that machine, but I was getting the impression that Clara wanted to see it, too. "Yes, of course. What about you, Marlie? Want a look?"

"Certainly, if it's not too much trouble."

Clara's eyes sparkled. "What harm could come from taking a quick look, right? But we really should hurry, before the others get here."

She led us back to the main room and stopped near the wardrobe. I wondered if she was going to ask us to take off our robes, but instead, she placed her hand on the wall beside the cabinet and pushed, making the panel all the way down to the floorboard spring away, just like the pocketed bookshelves above.

"It's really quite a marvelous apparatus. You'll see." Clara pulled open the hidden door and stepped inside, where the rhythmic chug and hum grew louder without the wall to dull its sound. She pushed a bronze button on the other side of the threshold and a series of gas lamps ignited to illuminate a narrow corridor.

When Marlie and I followed her inside, I realized it only looked like a corridor because what I'd taken for a solid wall was actually the side of a massive cabinet that filled most of the room, leaving only a narrow path around its perimeter. On every side, the box was fitted with brass gauges, levers, and buttons, and a tangle of brass tubes that connected it to various spots along the ceiling.

Marlie ran her fingertips over the gleaming wood surface. "So, this thing-a-ma-jig is the reason Windsor had to send away our books?"

"Yes, Miss Carlisle, that is a fair summation, but the proper term for it is *psychrometer*."

At the sound of the man's voice, we whipped around to find an older man of portly proportions with dark marble eyes and gray whiskers standing in the open doorway. His baggy twill pants and workman's shirt marked him as a laborer, but there was the sharp tenor of authority in his voice.

"What it does," he continued, stepping inside and checking the readings on a gauge, "is to monitor and react to the level of moisture within the hall, so we are able to maintain optimal conditions to protect the ephemera of the Library and archival collections, with the ability to make special accommodation during the excessive moisture caused by the Converging Ceremony. That is why Windsor's books were brought here, and that is how we can ensure they will last many more generations to come."

Clara bowed her head. "I beg your pardon, Mr. Starwyck. Miss Carlisle and Miss Shackle were only curious to see your apparatus. Since they're our guests, I thought there'd be no harm—"

"Yes, yes, it's fine, Miss Bellington."

I could see the fear in Clara's eyes fade.

Mr. Starwyck stepped to a bank of switches and flipped several upward, then turned back to us. "She is a rather remarkable contraption, isn't she?" There was the distinct twinkle of pride in his eye. "But if you'll be so kind as to rejoin the others. I believe it's time for me to finish the preparations."

"Yes, sir. Of course." Clara hurried us by Mr. Starwyck, who had moved to a brass panel and was flipping more switches and turning knobs as the machine's whirring, chugging, and churning quieted. "There, now." He leaned back and nodded with approval. "That's better."

He turned and saw the three of us still lingering in the doorway, watching him. "Please proceed, ladies. There's nothing more to see here."

CHAPTER THREE

MY LEGS WOBBLED and my palms turned moist beneath my gloves as Clara, Marlie, and I stepped back into the main room of Fayte Hall. Could I have made a worse impression on Lucas's father?

I doubted it, and the way Clara stared at the ground and avoided my gaze only confirmed my fear. Still, there was nothing to be done about it now. While we were exploring the psychrometer, Fayte Guardians had been arriving for the ceremony. More than two dozen were already in robes and congregating near the hearth while others were still tugging on the garments. None of them, at least, seemed to be paying any attention to us.

All eyes were on the purple-robed Scryer as she parted a pair of blue velvet curtains to reveal the Balmoral Sanctum. Finally, something looked familiar.

Unlike everything else in this place, the Sanctum was a near replica of the one at Windsor Castle. The pale marble floor depicted the same circular braid of black inlaid stone. The curved walls were covered with tapestries, most featuring Druansha, Boudica, and the daughters. Even the translucent divining pool appeared the same. It stood at the back of the room, filling with its cascading mist that indicated the time for the Converging Ceremony was near.

Clara didn't lead us toward the pool, however. She made her way through the robed figures, and I followed, forcing myself to smile at those I recognized and even those I didn't. I turned to ask Marlie if she saw Lucas but discovered she'd wandered away. I found her standing at a glass curio case, examining a brass neck torc and a rosy hued crystal many times larger than the typical Faytling stone, larger even than Druansha's pendant. The small plaque read *Artifacts of Eithne, the Fayte Heir.*

"Why isn't this collection locked away in a museum somewhere?" Marlie said to me when I joined her. "It's marvelous. I had no idea the Order possessed such treasures."

"Yes. Astonishing." My flat tone didn't go unnoticed.

She frowned. "Do you realize how valuable these are? Do you know how much they're worth?"

"A lot?" I muttered.

Marlie sighed. "You're embarrassed, aren't you? About Mr. Starwyck."

I made a face. "I'm not embarrassed. We weren't doing anything wrong, not really."

She half chuckled. "We weren't supposed to be there. Clara said so."

"I guess." I left it at that because she was right, and I didn't want to admit it. I *was* embarrassed. Maybe not for being where I shouldn't, but certainly for getting caught. I glanced around, looking for some way to change the subject and realized Clara had disappeared from view.

"I don't think he was angry," Marlie said, trying to make me feel better.

I searched the gaps in the crowd for Clara, but it wasn't easy in that sea of identical indigo robes. "How do you know?"

She shook her head in the way that said, "You're blowing things out of proportion."

Maybe I was, but I couldn't help it. I knew all too well how difficult it could be to turn around a bad impression.

She leaned close and dropped her voice. "If you want to apologize, now might be the time."

"What do you mean?"

She didn't have to answer, however, because a familiar voice boomed through the crowd.

"Ah, there you are. I've been looking for you, Miss Shackle."

I blushed as the gathering pulled apart and Mr. Starwyck approached, now covered like everyone else in an indigo robe. "I didn't mean to run you off. You merely caught me off guard, though I suppose I shouldn't have been surprised. Mrs. Crossey told me you were curious about the old records. I guess that curiosity extends into other areas as well."

If his voice hadn't been so cheerful, I might have crumpled on the spot. Still, I found it difficult to form a reply, so I merely smiled.

Luckily, Clara chose that moment to reappear.

"Mr. Starwyck, you should know Jane has been an immense help in the kitchen, just as Mrs. Crossey said she would be."

I appreciated her compliment, even if I wasn't certain it was true.

He clasped his fingers over his rotund belly and leaned back on his heels. He returned only an enigmatic stare until a smile spread slowly across his face. "Good to hear, and I must say, I've heard similar reports from my son. He's been singing Miss Shackle's praises since he returned."

Lucas was singing my praises? I looked away to hide my flushing cheeks. Was Lucas near? He must be, but where?

"I do hope you're enjoying your stay with us," the elder Starwyck continued.

"I am, sir. Thank you." Maybe Marlie was right. Maybe he wasn't angry.

"If there's anything you need or any way I can be of assistance, consider me at your service." He glanced past me and seemed to catch someone's eye before turning back. "If you'll excuse me, I must attend to a bit of business. It was a pleasure making your acquaintance, officially, however. I do hope you'll enjoy your stay with us."

"Thank you, sir. The pleasure was mine." I offered the deepest curtsy I could manage.

He tipped his head and moved around me, leaving an exaggerated gulf between us.

Had Mrs. Crossey told him of my visions as well? Surely, she would have, and now he was showing me the kindness of accommodation. But why was everyone staring? Fresh insecurity washed over me. I leaned toward Clara. "Why are they all looking at me? Did I do something wrong?"

She surveyed the room. "They're just curious. The High Councilor rarely socializes before a ceremony, especially with anyone outside of the Council. You should be flattered."

My hand flew to my lips. "He's your High Councilor?"

At Windsor, the Supreme Elder outranked the High Councilor, but here there was no higher authority in the Fayte Order. So, why hadn't Lucas mentioned it? He had told me about losing his mother when he was younger, but he'd never mentioned anything about his father.

"Clara, bring Jane forward." It was the voice of a young woman, and it was coming from the Sanctum. The Scryer had taken her place at the divining pool, her hood still pulled low.

"Always so bossy," Clara muttered under her breath. Then, more loudly, she said, "We're coming," and she nudged me forward.

When we reached the pool, the Scryer pulled back her hood. I recognized Clara's sister, Ada, instantly.

If she noticed my shock, she didn't show it. Instead, she looked meekly at the figure who had joined her on the other side. It was the elder Mr. Starwyck, whose paunch gave him away despite the low hood that now left only the gray whiskers on his chin visible.

"Shall we begin?" she asked him.

He responded with a solemn nod.

Ada gripped the pool's rim. "It's time, everyone."

As the Fayte Guardians shuffled into a circle that followed the floor's inlaid braid, I searched for Lucas. It was impossible, though. With their hoods up and eyes cast down, I couldn't get a good look at anyone. Those who hadn't already pulled their Faytlings from beneath their collars did so now, and all those crystals glimmered with a soft lavender glow.

The Scryer held out her arms. "Let us begin."

At once, the Guardians raised their hands over the pool and lowered their fingertips into the mist rising from its surface.

I was still looking for Lucas. With a gentle poke of her elbow, Clara nudged me to pay attention.

Quickly, I tugged off my gloves and tucked them between the opening of the robe and into my skirt pocket before reaching into the basin. A sudden nervousness made me pause before I touched the water. I hadn't communicated with Druansha since my initiation nearly two months before, and I wasn't sure what would happen.

Mrs. Crossey had explained it might be different. Although the purpose of the pool was to create a connection between the Fayte and Druansha, she didn't always choose to communicate the same way. Sometimes a message was felt by all, and sometimes only by the Scryers. In some instances, a message was communicated solely to the Master Scryer in Windsor, and in those cases, she would convey it through the Convergence connection to the First Scryers of the outer regions. If the message was unclear, it would be left to the respective High Councilors and Supreme Elder for interpretation.

Since I'd only participated in two Convergings, there was still much I didn't know. For instance, when I'd participated in my first ceremony at Windsor, my touch had turned the white mist a dark violet. Mrs. Crossey had received a strong message from Druansha, which she'd attributed to my presence, but she didn't know why or how. No one did.

As my fingertips hovered over the water now, a tingling surged through me. But was it real or my imagination? There was only one way to find out, so I lowered my hands. At the touch of the cool water, the white mist changed to a vibrant amethyst hue.

Gasps erupted around me, and the whispers began.

"It's true."

"Just like they said."

"What does it mean?"

I closed my eyes and pretended not to hear. I focused on swaying my fingers through the water in gentle figure eights, like everyone else, and waited for the message.

As the moments passed, it occurred to me that Mrs. Crossey and the other Windsor Fayte Guardians were gathered around that divining pool, just as we were here. I wondered how she was managing as Master Scryer now that she was also Supreme Elder, yet even before the thought was complete, my mind drifted away from it.

Hazy images flickered through my thoughts. Some happy. Some ordinary. Pictures and words and feelings all wrapped up in the mundane tasks of caring for the castle and its occupants. Somehow, I felt strangely free and completely untethered by form, as light as a breath of air.

Then I discovered I could move. I could roam! Without hesitation, I glided through the doorway and through the Fayte tunnel until I was back in the castle. The wall should have been an impediment, but I passed through it as easily as a cloud, and soon I was back in the kitchen. There was a guard sitting on a stool in a corner, asleep at his post, snoring with his chin to his chest. I passed through another wall and found myself hovering above the vast western lawn. Perhaps the darkness should have obscured my vision, but I could see everything, and the sight spurred me on.

I floated to the woodlands, where an elk herd gathered among the trees. As I neared, something spooked them—was it me? When they darted off toward the denser forest, I followed, exhilarated by their speed and grace. I followed until a front of clouds blocked the moon and the stars above, and the temperature dropped to a near-freezing degree.

It was exciting to travel this way, in spirit form. It certainly wasn't like before. My first attempt had lasted only seconds, and I'd become too weak to continue. The second had lasted several minutes, but still my energy waned. That I felt no weakness now had to be a sign I was finally mastering the skill. I only wished I could outpace the gathering darkness.

Above me, the clouds were closing in, but when I looked, I saw it wasn't clouds at all. The blanket of black crept toward me, like a shadow stretched across the sky.

A voice pierced the silence.

There you are.

In a flash, the forest, the lawn, the kitchen, and the tunnel sped past me in a blur. When I could feel myself back within my skin, I yanked my fingers from the pool and opened my eyes.

"What's wrong?" Clara stared at me, startled.

Had she sensed it, too? Had any of them? I searched around the basin, but every head was still bowed. No one seemed to notice me at all. In a whisper, I asked her: "Did you feel it?" My heart raced; I fought to breathe.

"Feel what? The water?"

It was a soft shade of lavender. Nothing of the darker hue remained.

I could see her confusion. She hadn't heard him. She hadn't sensed him at all. I searched around the pool again, and except for Clara, no one noticed my distress. Not even Marlie.

He'd spoken only to me.

"I don't know what happened," I whispered. "Maybe I'm not feeling well." I rubbed my fingers and shook the wetness from them, wishing I could rid myself of every drop, as if that could remove the memory of that haunting voice.

Krol.

But how could it be? Druansha had banished him. She'd told me I was safe.

What if he's back?

That tiny voice wasn't his. It was my own. Shivers raced along my arms, and I hugged myself, afraid to touch anything. Afraid of everything.

Marlie opened her eyes and leaned toward me. "Are you all right? Do you need a break?"

I nodded, eager for a reprieve. "I do. I absolutely do."

Ada cleared her throat, making it known that we were disrupting the ceremony.

"If you don't wish to continue," she said through gritted teeth, "please leave."

Her eyes gleamed. She wanted me gone.

"Yes, thank you," I mumbled and stepped back from the circle.

"You don't have to go," Clara whispered before slanting a grimace at her sister.

"No, she's right," I said. "I need to leave right now."

CHAPTER FOUR

NO ONE SAID a word or tried to stop me as I rushed from the Sanctum, eager to put distance between me and that divining pool. I slipped through the velvet drapes, which had been pulled closed when the ceremony began, and sought the solitude of the empty main room.

Soft footfalls behind me signaled I wasn't alone. I should have known Marlie would follow. I turned to assure her I was fine but found myself standing face-to-face with Lucas. My words faded to nothing at the sight of him, as did every thought in my head.

"You?" I'm sure I sounded like a proper lunatic, but after what had happened in the Sanctum, I didn't completely trust my senses. I didn't trust anything, yet that didn't stop the barrage of emotions churning inside me. Happiness to finally see him, yes, but a large dose of doubt and uncertainty as well. I still couldn't reconcile why he had kept so much from me.

His cheeks turned a deep crimson that even the shadows beneath his hood couldn't hide. Nervously, he pushed back the indigo shroud and raked his fingers through his chestnut hair. "I wanted to be sure you were all right. That you weren't going to faint or something."

Now it was my turn to blush. Not so long ago, I'd awakened from a faint on a hillside beyond the Windsor Castle wall to find him standing over me. That had been the second time I'd fainted in as many days.

"I don't know what's wrong with me," I said. It was the truth; I didn't understand any of it. "Maybe I just need some fresh air."

"Maybe." He glanced back at the velvet curtains. "It's a lot to take in. All of this." He glanced up at the soaring pillars, the chairs and tables, and all the glass cases filled with Fayte treasures.

My composure returned as I followed his gaze around the great hall. "This is such a remarkable place. Clara told me you and your father oversaw its construction. It's an incredible accomplishment."

He scuffed the toe of his black boot along the border of an ornate rug. "It was mostly my father's doing. The part I played was small."

. "Still impressive. I had no idea you possessed such skill. You must have been bored silly to be stuck in the Windsor mews with the horses when you were used to work like this."

He stared into the flowers and vines drawn in wool beneath our feet. "I'm happy to be where I'm needed. I had a job to do at Windsor, or so I thought."

"Right." I bristled at the memory that he'd been there with orders to spy on me.

It had been difficult to learn someone at Windsor believed me capable of harming anyone, let alone the Queen, and it had been even more difficult to hear that truth from the person I'd believed to be guilty of that crime.

Learning we were both wrong had been a relief as well as a heartache. We'd discovered in due course that Mr. Bailey had concocted his scheme because he'd believed himself cheated by Druansha when he wasn't installed as

Supreme Elder when that position became vacant. The man's desire for power and revenge made him weak and easy prey for Krol.

"I also wanted to apologize for not checking on you sooner," he said.

Had he missed me, then? The thought shot through me like a lightning bolt, yet I tried to feign indifference. "Why should you? I'm sure you've been busy."

He struggled for words, and I could swear my heart cracked right in half. This time I welcomed the sound of footsteps, many of them, headed toward us from the other side of the curtain. All at once, a stream of Fayte Guardians filed out of the Sanctum. Some were tucking their Faytlings back beneath their collars, others were chatting with neighbors, but one familiar face walked directly toward us.

When she approached, she hooked a lock of pale hair behind her ear before sliding a hand onto Lucas's shoulder. "I wondered where you went," she cooed at him. When she smiled at me, it held none of the warmth I'd seen in the Servants' Hall the day before. "Hello, Jane. It's nice to see you again."

I returned the greeting, though it was difficult not to be distracted by her hand on his shoulder. They obviously knew each and well, but he'd never mentioned her. Then again, he hadn't mentioned so many things.

Lucas stepped to the side to release himself from her touch. "Did you need something?" Irritation thinned his voice.

One of her eyebrows arched over her gray-slate eyes. "I do, actually. Your father wants to see you in the Sanctum."

Your father. Not *our* father. So, not a sister. A long shot, but I couldn't help but hope.

"Tell him I'll be there in a moment. I'm having a word with Jane." His jaw tightened, and his lips curled in.

Ivy's hand returned to his shoulder and made its way

up over the bare skin of his neck, a caress far too intimate for a relative, or a friend, or anyone in a public place for that matter. I looked away as the uncomfortable truth became apparent.

"I'll relay the message. Shall we take a turn around the garden in the moonlight, like we usually do?"

She glanced at me as she ended her question, and I knew without a doubt it had been for my benefit. Again, she stroked his neck before letting her fingertips drift back to her side.

"Not tonight." He stared straight ahead, avoiding me or her, or both; I couldn't tell. "It's late, and I need to get an early start in the wood shop."

"You work too hard, darling," she cooed again. "But then, you always have, haven't you? I'll see you soon." She touched his shoulder again lightly and gave me an obligatory smile before slipping away.

When she was gone, I waited for him to say something, but he only stared at the fire crackling in the hearth.

"She seems nice," I said when the silence became too much. Every part of me wanted to know what she was to him, but I had no right to ask. Instead, I waited for him to speak.

After a long, tense moment of staring at the flames, he pulled back his shoulders and opened his mouth as if to say something, but another movement of the curtain stopped him.

His father emerged, his lips dipped sharply in a frown. Behind him, I could see Ivy gazing out, looking sheepish.

"Lucas!" James Starwyck's voice boomed. The fiery glint in his eye and that furrowed brow were a far cry from the amiable expression he'd worn before the ceremony.

Lucas's shoulders drooped under an invisible weight. His eyes lost their luster. "You'll have to excuse me."

He covered the floor in long strides, his back and arms as stiff as I'd ever seen them, and followed his father back into the Sanctum without looking back, not even once.

~ ~ ~

Marlie left me in silence as we returned to our room. She didn't speak until she was in her nightgown and braiding her hair at the oval mirror that hung over the washbasin. "You missed the Lady's message. Aren't you curious what it was?"

After the shock of Krol invading my thoughts and the encounter with Lucas and Ivy that followed, the Lady's message had not been foremost on my mind. Judging from Marlie's sly grin, however, the news had been good.

"Of course, I am. What did she say?"

"Her Majesty is coming! We're to expect a visit before the next New Moon. Isn't that wonderful? It's been a bit dreary without them, don't you think?"

"That's all she said?"

Marlie stared at me through the mirror. "Were you expecting something else? Did *you* get a message?"

I gnawed my lip. I didn't dare tell her the truth. Honestly, I wasn't even sure what the truth was. As she watched me, my mind raced for an answer. That's when I noticed the smell. I lifted my nose and sniffed. "Are you wearing perfume?"

She twisted around. "Perfume? Oh, you must be smelling the basil. I found a patch near the oaks beyond the western fields. I couldn't find any in the kitchen garden, which is a shame because it's perfect for sniffles and sneezes and all kinds of little things. I snipped a bit to have on hand." She opened a drawer and pointed to a small bundle wrapped in one of her white handkerchiefs.

Marlie's ability to remember the healing properties of plants made her useful in the Windsor kitchen, where she always had a well-stocked supply at her fingertips. She also had a knack for persuading cooks to incorporate her healing herbs into their sauces and stocks to enhance their flavor. Only those who were also Fayte Guardians understood her ulterior motives.

When we'd arrived at Balmoral, she was quick to find fault with the kitchen garden here. She complained about the lack of white willow bark, a particular favorite for pain relief; the scarcity of peppermint, which she often recommended for aiding digestion, muscle aches, and vigor; and the weakness of the thyme, which she claimed rendered it useless as a balm for sore throats and coughs. She'd made herself so disagreeable those first two days, it was no wonder she'd been moved upstairs.

Still, I wasn't surprised to hear she'd been scouring the grounds for wild herbs to supplement her own supply, which she kept in a drawer that was now crammed with bundles of herbs like this one.

She ran a gentle fingertip over the new addition before tying a pink ribbon around the end of her braid and flipping it over her shoulder.

"I saw you talking to Lucas." She hesitated and I wondered if she'd seen the awkward exchange with Ivy as well. She lowered herself to the edge of her bed and picked lint from her gown. "I know it must have come as a shock."

"I suppose so." I didn't want to talk about Lucas. What I wanted to do was crawl under the covers and put the whole day behind me, but I forced myself through my usual bedtime routine. The hair brushing, the teeth cleaning, the tidying up. "It was nice to see him again. He seems well."

She cocked her head to the side. "You don't have to pretend with me."

I swallowed hard. I wasn't sure what she meant, so I continued to peel away my clothes until I was down to my muslin chemise.

She wasn't dissuaded. "Just because I pretended not to

notice what you two were up to during the journey doesn't mean I didn't know what was going on. You have every right to be upset."

I pulled the pins from the tight knot of hair atop my head and let the dark waves fall around my shoulders. "Why should I be upset?" I tried to scoff, but the sound lodged awkwardly in my throat.

"Because he never told you about *her*, did he? I don't recall him ever mentioning he was engaged."

Time slowed to a crawl. Lucas and Ivy were engaged? Somehow, I lost the ability to move or speak.

I don't know if Marlie expected a response, but I was sure my flaming cheeks and neck told her all she needed to know. Instead of answering, I stared at my hands, still protected by the ivory leather and balled into fists in my lap.

"I only found out myself tonight. Clara mentioned it when we saw you talking to them. Clara says they were betrothed more than a year ago."

It couldn't be true. Marlie must be mistaken. He would have said something. He wouldn't have let me go on the way I had if he'd made that promise to another.

"I'm so sorry to be the one to tell you." She reached out to put a comforting hand on my knee but pulled it back. Even now, sometimes she forgot about the visions.

"Are you absolutely sure?" My voice broke. I couldn't continue.

"I wish I wasn't, but I am. Quite sure."

I rose from the bed and walked the length of our spartan room. I didn't want her comfort. I didn't want her pity. I didn't want any of this. If she thought I'd be angry or hurt, she was wrong. I didn't feel anything. Whatever I thought I'd felt for Lucas Starwyck was only a gaping black hole of nothing.

A moment ago, the room had been unbearably hot, but now I shivered in my chemise. I turned to Marlie. "I appreciate you telling me. I know it couldn't have been easy, but it's fine. I'm quite all right. If you don't mind, I'm going to try to get some sleep. It's been a long day."

She gave me a funny look, like she wasn't sure if she should believe me, but she didn't try to stop me as I pulled back my bedcovers, slipped beneath them, and turned toward the wall so she couldn't see my face.

"Are you sure you're all right?" Her voice was small and uncertain.

"Don't be silly," I answered. "Of course, I am." I tried to keep a smile in my voice even as my fingertips curled into my palms and sliced painful crescents into my skin.

CHAPTER FIVE

I DID NOT drift off to sleep. Not after an hour, not even after two. I lay there in the fuzzy space between consciousness and dreams, replaying every conversation I'd ever had with Lucas Starwyck and every tender moment, searching for something that hinted at his relationship with Ivy Coombs. My anger doubled when I came up empty and tripled when I realized he'd given me no reason to believe he harbored anything more than friendship for me. Not really. How could I have been so blind?

I can give you what you want.

The voice startled me. It was Krol.

Or had I slipped into a dream?

Not a dream, my dear. We are connected, you and I.

I bolted upright and swung my feet to the floor. I needed to feel solid ground beneath me. I needed to break this spell.

My movements must have awakened Marlie because I heard her bedcovers rustle. "What's wrong?" she mumbled.

"Nothing. Just a bad dream. Go back to sleep."

Whatever she replied, it was muffled by her blankets,

and I heard her roll over.

At least one of us could sleep. At the rate my heart was pounding, I wouldn't be shutting my eyes again any time soon.

I stared at the shadows in the darkness. If I stayed here, I'd only have my thoughts to keep me company, and they weren't proving to be good company at all. "I'm going for a walk," I whispered, though I suspected Marlie had already fallen back asleep. I slipped out of bed, grabbed my boots, my gloves, and coat, and tiptoed out of the room.

On my way to the kitchen, I tried to convince myself the voice I'd heard wasn't Krol—not in my room and not during the Converging Ceremony. It was my own imagination. My own fears, surely.

I repeated the refrain again and again, but it didn't work. Deep in my heart, in the darkest corners of awareness, I knew the truth.

Krol had found me.

That frightened me to my core, but what truly terrified me was the possibility he was telling the truth: that I *was* part of him.

The thought almost dropped me to my knees. I struggled to breathe. I needed air, fresh air, so I set off down the dark corridor toward the kitchen courtyard.

At the door, I peered out, checking for guards. None were in sight, which wasn't surprising. Their rounds were spotty at best when the royal family wasn't in residence.

Emboldened, I let myself out and pressed my back against the hard wood as the night chill gripped me. It was cold but not freezing, and the nearly moonless sky glittered like a sea of sparkling stars. I closed my eyes and inhaled the crisp woodsy smell that was so different from Windsor. A reminder even in the darkness that thick forests blanketed the nearby hills.

The guards would be making their rounds eventually, so I set off along the pathway that wound through small patches of herbs and vegetables toward the outer gate that opened to the fields. I hurried to avoid being seen and to warm my blood, sticking to the shadows as best I could.

When I emerged from the castle grounds, I set a course for the tree ridge, where the guards weren't likely to venture. I hurried, eager to put distance between me and the residence, the Fayte Guardians, and, I hoped, Krol. Eager to put it all behind me.

Back at Windsor, when there was trouble, it was my habit to seek comfort outdoors, in the wild spaces and brisk English air. That's where I could always find my faithful companion, my dragonfly. No matter what else was falling apart, I could always count on her.

Despite Marlie and Mrs. Crossey and all the friends I'd made, I still longed for that little visitor. Druansha had said we were still friends, but nothing felt the same. She was the Lady of the Fayte, a timeless creature I hardly understood and far more powerful than I could even imagine. Who was she, really? *What* was she? It seemed certain she was what superstitious souls called fairies or fae, the magical beings who roamed these lands in the time before men. All I knew for certain, however, was she was much more than my dragonfly, which meant she had never truly been *my* dragonfly at all.

Tonight, I felt that loss as keenly as I had the day she'd revealed her true form.

My cheeks ached with the chill of cold tears streaming down my face, and my breath came in heaves and gasps. Only then did I realize I was running across the fields and along the edge of the woodlands that covered the western hills. I ran until my legs nearly gave out along the dirt path I followed.

What was I running from? I didn't even know. Krol? Lucas and Ivy? My own stupidity? It didn't matter. I wanted to run until I had no more breath and not an ounce of strength left in my limbs. When I finally stopped,

I could hardly stand. My heart pounded, and my ears buzzed. Slowly, my breathing eased, and the pounding lessened, but the buzzing continued.

That strange buzz…

A familiar buzz…

I glanced up, searching the shadows for a moth or swarm of midges. I waved my hands to scare away whatever it was or at least to send it off in another direction.

Then I saw her. Flying in a lazy figure eight just beyond my reach, between me and the edge of the oak grove.

I rubbed my eyes and blinked. Was it my imagination? Was it a trick? It certainly looked like her, flying in that same old meandering way. The starlight limned the silvery needle of her body and made her gossamer wings glow with a soft iridescence. Her violet eyes held me, greeting me and beckoning me to follow as she darted toward the trees and back again.

"Is it really you?" I knew the answer but still some part of me needed the confirmation.

The answer came back with crystalline clarity: "Follow me."

She must have sensed my hesitation for she darted again toward the trees, urging me forward. "Trust me," she said in her way.

I wanted to so badly. I took a deep breath and stepped into the wood.

Following her, however, was easier said than done. I hurried behind for several paces without knowing where she was going, then she began to glow with a lavender light. Just her insect form at first, then the brightness stretched above her and below until it formed a swirling column of shimmering color, sparkling pink, lavender, and purple. When it dissolved, she stood before me. The Ancient One in her ageless womanly form, with white flowing hair and a diaphanous gown. She floated inches above the ground until she touched down with the grace of a falling leaf.

"There, that's better," she said, giving her arms and hair a gentle shake. She gazed down upon me from her towering height. "And you. It is good to see you, Jane Shackle. I searched for you at the Converging. Why were you not there?"

She didn't know? I could see it in the placid way she looked at me. She had absolutely no idea why I'd fled.

Perhaps I *had* imagined the encounter. My hope surged.

"I was..." I stopped without finishing. A tiny inner voice whispered, *Don't tell her. It would be unwise.*

Was that his voice? Was it my own? I stared at her, wide eyed and mute, not knowing what to do.

"You were what, my dear?"

"I was... not feeling well, so I excused myself." It was almost true. I watched her, looking for signs of suspicion.

She only glanced up at the horizon with a hint of a smile. "Yes, and it is such a lovely night, isn't it? Quite nice to be out. Are you feeling better?"

"Yes, thank you." I forced myself to think of nothing, not Krol, not the ceremony, not even Lucas or Ivy. If she didn't already know what had transpired, some instinct urged me not to let her find it in my thoughts. I pushed everything down, far out of reach.

"I'm glad to hear it, but I'm afraid I've come with a warning." There was a sharpness to her words.

"Oh?" *Don't think. Don't think.*

She frowned and looked toward the trees. "It's a difficult matter, unfortunately. It's about my brother."

My blood ran cold. "But he's banished. You told me so. You said he can't return to this world."

She toyed with the silvery trim adorning her bell sleeves. "That's true, but he isn't where he's supposed to be. It shouldn't be possible, and it concerns me."

My eyes rounded. If he wasn't where he was supposed

to be, where was he?

Druansha touched her throat, her fingers finding their way to the purple crystal pendant upon her neck, the one her brother had stolen from her and, with it, her power to alter forms and travel between realms. "I've looked for him, of course, but there's no sign of him anywhere."

I tried to swallow, but my mouth was dry. I couldn't speak.

Worry shadowed her face before giving way to a smile. "He may have warded himself somehow, though wards have never been his strength. I can think of no other explanation. I only wondered if you've seen or heard something."

Fear lanced my heart.

"What is it, Jane?" Her chin lifted, and her gaze measured every movement.

"Will he come for me?" My voice cracked.

Her elegant shoulders slumped. "I have no reason to think so."

It wasn't as reassuring as I'd hoped, but it was something. I swallowed hard and marshaled my courage. If I didn't ask now, I may never have another chance. "He told me he was my father. When we were in the Gray Woods, before I grabbed your crystal." The words rushed out in a torrent, and for a moment, I was back in that place. That awful, nightmarish landscape that was not the Brightlands or the human world, but a strange in-between place. The grayness of it wasn't so much a scarcity of color but a scarcity of life: devoid of light and comfort and hope. Especially hope.

Again, I could see that forest of hulking trees that gripped the ground with talon-sharp roots and scratched the sky with bare, spiny fingers. Every step was a descent into deeper misery. It was a place for the forgotten and the shunned, and the ones with nowhere else to go.

Below me, the ground seemed to shift. It took all my

strength to remain steady. "Is it true?" I asked Druansha. "Is he…?"

She didn't answer at first, but her eyes shone with a fiery radiance that brightened by degrees. "My brother is a liar," she said at last. "He had no business saying that to you. He deceives, and he manipulates. You must never trust him."

The intensity of her words startled me, but it was what she didn't say that shook me to my core. She didn't say he wasn't my father.

She composed herself again. "You can be sure I'll do everything I can to keep you safe."

"I know." Even as I said the words, I knew I didn't believe them. She despised her brother, and if she knew I was his daughter, surely that colored her feelings for me as well. Perhaps that's why I hadn't seen her since my initiation. New doubts coursed through me. She had pretended to be my friend for years. If she was deceiving me now, would I even know?

Druansha twitched and then gently twisted her neck and her shoulders one way and then another as if trying to wriggle free of something.

"Is something wrong?" I asked.

Her eyes opened on me, and she shook her shoulders once more. "I'd hoped to have more time, but the air is too dry. I cannot stay. You must return to the castle. Stay there. Stay safe."

Before I could respond, she vanished in a flash of light. Not even my dragonfly remained.

Since there was nothing left to do but follow her warning, I hurried back to the castle and thought about what she'd said. Yet, even as I tried, it was what she hadn't said that vexed me.

Could it be true? Was Krol my father?

I replayed her words again, searching for something to give me hope.

I came up empty.

Bile rose in my throat and doubled me over, making me retch what was left of my evening stew onto the grass. Shame and anger washed over me in waves. When my gut had emptied, I stood again and whispered through my tears, "Please tell me it isn't true."

There was no answer. I listened for the buzz of a dragonfly. I looked for that silvery presence. Nothing.

Slowly, grudgingly, I made my way back to the castle. As I reached for the door to the castle's kitchen, her words came back to me: *My brother is a liar.*

I truly hoped he was. It was the only hope I had left.

CHAPTER SIX

FOR THE NEXT few days, I stuck close to the kitchen and tried not to think about Krol, Druansha, or the Gray Woods. There was little I could do about any of them, so I focused on the problem closer at hand: avoiding Lucas. It was easy enough, and when I discovered Ivy in the Servants' Hall, I pretended I'd forgotten something at the stove. I excused myself and never returned.

If Clara suspected something was wrong, she didn't say so. But then, she'd been quieter than usual and more distracted, as though her mind were elsewhere. She didn't even ask if I'd gone back to the Library.

That was fine with me.

Instead of thinking about Lucas or hunting through old records, I immersed myself in work. I managed to master a decent semolina porridge—no lumps and a touch of sweetness. I also memorized every dish I helped Clara make, from the simple cucumber sandwiches, jam, and biscuits that were put out for afternoon tea to the weekday stews and Sunday roasts delivered to the Servants' Hall.

One day when Clara was especially complimentary about a pheasant pie I'd reproduced perfectly on my second try, I mustered the courage to ask a question I'd been harboring for days. "How is it you were promoted from maid to cook so quickly? Mrs. Crossey said she'd been a kitchen maid for decades before she was elevated to cook."

Clara grinned as she wiped flour from her hands. "I wouldn't put myself in the same league as Mrs. Crossey. You forget, Balmoral isn't Windsor. There's a world of difference between us."

"Still, what you've managed is quite admirable."

She stared at me so long I wondered if she'd respond at all. Finally, after the weight of her scrutiny had made my skin prickly, she said, "You learn quickly; that will serve you well. You also follow instructions. But I'll tell you what helped me get to where I am, or at least what I think helped me: I worked hard and learned the way things were done, but I didn't always do exactly as I was told."

She must have sensed my confusion because she laughed.

"Do you think I'm joking? I assure you, I'm not. There was one occasion in particular when the Queen was in residence and her cook fell ill. We were short-staffed that morning, so I was asked to make her breakfast porridge. I was told exactly what to do: Boil the water, add the semolina, a pat of butter, and a touch of salt. Nothing more." She paused with a sheepish look. "I've never been much for porridge myself, however, and I've found I can only tolerate it if I add stewed apples and cinnamon. So, that's what I did for the Queen. I made her the kind of porridge I preferred to eat."

"How did you get away with it? I mean, not following orders. Didn't anyone see what you'd done?"

"Since we were shorthanded, people were rushing to get things done, and no one was paying attention to my porridge. The bowl was delivered under a cloche; no one saw it until it was served to the Queen. I suppose everyone in her breakfast room saw it wasn't her usual porridge. The maids, footmen, the Queen's companions. When a note was passed down later that morning, I expected to be ripped to shreds by the House Steward. But that's not what happened. The note wasn't a complaint; it was a compliment. It seems the Queen had always taken her porridge in the same bland way because that's the only way it had ever been given to her. A few days later, I was promoted. That was about six months ago."

I sank onto a stool beside the worktable. "So, are you saying I should have added something to the pheasant pie? More thyme or sage, perhaps?"

"Not at all. Your pie is lovely the way it is. My point is simply to remember there is more than one way to do something. Just because it has always been done one way, doesn't mean *you* have to do it that way. When you're ready and if you're inclined, you might introduce a change that makes it better."

"Or worse," I said, which made her laugh again.

"Yes, that's also a possibility. Perhaps I've been lucky."

For the next few hours, I washed leeks and peeled carrots for a mutton stew and thought about what she'd said. How difficult could it be to improve upon a dish or two? As I watched her slice cucumbers thin as parchment for tea sandwiches, I wondered about adding radish slices for a peppery taste and a touch of color. Or, maybe mixing basil with the butter instead of dill.

I considered several options, but I kept coming back to the basil, probably because I'd always been partial to it and, since it wasn't grown in the kitchen garden, it might catch the Queen's attention.

It would be tricky getting my hands on some, though. Marlie prohibited me from tampering with her beloved bundles, but maybe I could persuade her to show me where the wild basil grew, so I could collect my own.

I didn't think any more about it until late afternoon passed into evening, when Clara asked if I'd mind cleaning up early. I took it as a sign that I shouldn't wait for Marlie. Since there was still at least an hour of daylight left, I could visit the grove and search for the basil myself.

When I emerged outdoors, the sun had only begun to slide toward the western horizon. I headed toward the line of trees and searched the low brush for a basil patch. Yet the deeper I moved into the grove, the thicker the tree canopy became and the more difficult it was to identify the plants I passed.

I found nettles and brambles, ferns and mosses. But where was the basil?

I'd been walking at least a quarter of an hour when I decided Marlie couldn't possibly have come so far. I headed back toward the castle, keeping my eye on the ground in case I'd missed something. Soon, however, I came to the edge of the River Dee, instead of the castle. Somehow, I'd turned myself around.

After walking so long, I wasn't even sure which direction I was going, and what was left of the sun was retreating into darkness. Using tree moss as my guide, I reasoned I would be moving in an easterly direction if I kept it on my left side. It would have to lead me back to the castle eventually.

I walked for several minutes, but the tree canopy grew denser. Was I walking in circles? Somewhere in the distance an owl hooted, and I heard the crunch of dead leaves under foot.

The crunch wouldn't have been so alarming if I hadn't been standing still.

Fear paralyzed me. Was it him? Was he here?

As twilight dimmed to darkness, panic overshadowed rational thought. Should I run? But where? I'd lost all sense of direction. I considered calling out for Druansha's help, but no, not after our last encounter. I couldn't count on her, not anymore. She wasn't my dragonfly. I wasn't even sure she was my friend. So, I sought the only help I still trusted: my Faytling.

Pulling the pendant from beneath my collar, I willed it to light my way. I couldn't have strayed far, I reasoned. I just needed to orient myself and figure out why I was getting so turned around.

Slowly, its lavender light emerged.

That's when I heard voices.

My hope surged, and I was about to call out for help when I spied three lanterns. I should have been relieved to see them, but I wasn't. The tiny hairs on the back of my neck rose and not from the cold night air. I lowered my Faytling and extinguished its light with a silent command.

Instead of calling out, I moved toward their light like a moth to a flame, trying my best to stay silent. Each time I stepped on a twig or a brittle leaf, I stopped and listened to be sure the sound hadn't alerted them.

The conversation, which I could almost hear now, didn't pause. There was a man, older with a deep voice, and a younger woman. No, two women. Was that Clara? Yes, as I strained to listen, I heard her distinct cadence. As they neared, I could make out their words.

"Do you see what I mean, sir? The trees are dying. It was just this one when I noticed it a few days ago, but the rot has spread. At least five are infected now, all here in a circle. What's even more troubling is that I believe this spot is directly above Fayte Hall. Clara thinks so, too. It's a strange coincidence, don't you think?"

"It's certainly not a good sign." That was Mr. Starwyck, I could hear it now. "Why didn't you mention it before?"

"It didn't seem necessary until I saw how it spread, but I did tell my sister. Didn't I, Clara?"

Something affirming was mumbled back.

"Since the Lady didn't mention anything about it during the Converging Ceremony, we didn't think it was a problem. But this morning, I saw this. Something must be wrong."

I peered around the oak trunk that separated me from them, but all I saw was the faint glow of three lanterns and the silhouette of a tree that appeared darker than it should.

"You were right to bring your concerns to me. I've never seen anything like this. I'll consult the Council; perhaps someone has encountered it before. For now, let's not say anything to anyone else. There's no point alarming others, at least until we know more."

"Of course, sir," Ada said.

"I can feel a rain coming," he added. "We should get back inside. Go on ahead. I'll reset the ward."

A ward in these woods? That would explain why I'd wandered in circles.

As the girls moved away, Mr. Starwyck held back. From the shadows, I watched him pull a Faytling from beneath his collar and whisper something I couldn't hear.

When he turned back toward the castle, I followed so I wouldn't lose my way again but kept a discreet distance to remain out of sight.

Back in my room, I found Marlie already there.

She crinkled her nose when she saw me. "What happened to you? Your face is filthy, and look at that skirt! Is that mud?"

I found my reflection in the mirror. She was right. My cheeks were covered in grime, as were my sleeves and the bottom inches of my skirt. A few leaves and twigs had embedded themselves in my hair.

"Wait, are you hurt?" She lurched closer, ready to offer aid or comfort, or both.

I waved her off. "I'm fine. I went looking for the wild basil. Out in the western woods, like you said."

She frowned. "Why on earth would you do that?"

I shook my head. Honestly, I no longer knew.

CHAPTER SEVEN

THE MINUTES STRETCHED into hours, and the hours felt like days as I moved through my daily tasks. I simply couldn't focus. Or, to be more specific, I couldn't focus on my work. I was still angry about Lucas and Ivy, but even that took a distant second to my suspicion about that peculiar tree rot.

All morning I'd debated whether to ask Clara about it. Oaks dying overnight seemed like a problem for the groundskeeper, yet Ada had turned to Mr. Starwyck. Why?

The worry that kept scratching at the back of my thoughts was how much those ashen trunks and shriveled leaves had reminded me of the Gray Woods, the murky borderland between the Brightlands and the human world.

Was it Krol's doing? After his whispers at the divining pool, I had to wonder.

All day, I found myself glancing over my shoulder, searching the dark corners. But I decided I couldn't say anything to Clara. At best, she'd wonder why I'd be daft enough to wander about in the dark. At worst, she'd question my motives.

Besides, I'd already lied to Druansha. I didn't want to lie again to Clara. So, I kept my suspicions and my fears to myself.

I'd gotten so tangled up in my thoughts as I stood over the bubbling porridge on the stove that I didn't even notice the scorching smell. By the time Clara caught my eye and motioned me to take the pot off the fire, we both knew the batch was lost.

I didn't care. All I wanted to do was get through the day so I could get to Fayte Hall. For the first time since I'd arrived, I was eager to delve into the records to disprove Krol's claim on me. If Clara was right and they really kept everything, there had to be something on those shelves that would point to my parents.

That was the hope that got me out of bed in the morning and kept me going through the day.

When Clara finally released me from duties, I went to the Servants' Hall long enough to grab two biscuits then retired to my room. Since learning about Lucas and Ivy, I couldn't bring myself to eat with the others. I couldn't risk seeing either of them, and I certainly didn't want to see them together. So instead, I took whatever I could carry to my room and ate there.

Since it would be hours before I could get to the pantry without being noticed, I pulled out my memory box and removed my gloves.

By the time Marlie returned, well after the dinner hour, I'd handled every button, pin, and scrap of fabric I'd collected over the years for their fleeting glimpses of someone else's happy childhood, the small moments I'd stolen from others to ease the pain of losing my own past. Tonight wasn't about strolls down those conjured memory lanes, though. With my Faytling in hand, I was trying to see not only the past, but the present and future of the owners of these objects, as Mrs. Crossey had been training me to do.

"Are you making any progress?" Marlie asked when she saw the old tea caddy open on my bed and its contents spread out.

I was playing in a park on a warm summer day, a vision I'd acquired from a classmate at Chadwick Hollow by nicking a ribbon from her hair. I let the image fade before answering. "The Faytling helps, but I can still see only flashes of the present. The future eludes me completely."

"Don't give up." She made her way to the basin to wash her face before bed. "Mrs. Crossey said it would take time."

It had already been several weeks, and I was starting to wonder if my skills would ever improve.

She watched me through the looking glass. "Why are you still dressed? You haven't even touched the wash water."

"I'm going to… the pantry." I gave her a knowing look as I scooped up the trinkets and dropped them back into the caddy. "Did you notice if the kitchen is clear?"

My question didn't seem to surprise her. "It was almost empty when I left Servants' Hall." She grabbed the bun at the nape of her neck and pulled out a pin, letting her hair fall down her back. "I'll go, too. I can help."

I blanched. I didn't want company. Not tonight. "I should probably do this alone."

"Why? Two can accomplish more than one."

She was right, of course, and I knew she was curious about what I hoped to find. But if there was bad news to face, I wanted to confront it alone. My stomach churned, realizing I was already preparing myself for bad news.

"You're never going to tell me what you're looking for, are you?" she asked.

The question surprised me. It was the first time she'd ever asked so openly. It was the thing we never discussed, and I had no intention of starting now.

"Fine," she relented. "You can keep your secret. Can you at least tell me when you'll be back?"

"I'm not sure." I tucked my memory box into a drawer,

pulled on my gloves, and went to the door. "Don't wait up, though." I shut it softly behind me and hurried down the empty hallway toward the kitchen.

Keeping to the shadows, I reached the pantry without being seen. Marlie was right. Everyone was gone. There wasn't even a night cook on duty yet.

Before shutting myself inside the dark pantry, I pulled a candle from a drawer and lit it, then searched for the latch that would open the secret passage. I hadn't noticed how Clara had triggered it, but it was plain to see—now that I looked—that one of the corbels beneath the wall cabinets featured a dragon's head not unlike the one carved into the House Steward's mantel back at Windsor Castle. I pressed down on the snout, and as I'd hoped, it bent, activating a spring that pushed the cabinet away from the wall. On the other side was a passageway.

I hurried through and pulled the cabinet closed behind me. As quickly as I could, I descended the stairs, lighted the niche sconces, and followed the tunnel to the Fayte Hall door. Leaning my ear to the wood, I listened for any signs of occupants inside before opening it. No people sounds, only the soft whir and chug of the machine. Good. I preferred to avoid small talk or having to explain what I was doing.

I set the extinguished candle on the ground and pulled the Faytling from around my neck. When I pressed the talisman to the brass emblem, it settled quickly, and the familiar click released the door's lock to allow me in.

As before, the hall was lit inside by low-burning gas lamps that cast long shadows across the room.

I swallowed and felt the weight of being alone in this strange and incredible place. Perhaps I should have let Marlie join me. But no, whatever truth awaited me, I needed to face alone.

There was also the chance I'd find nothing relevant in the records at all. I suppose I had to prepare for that possibility as well.

I gazed up to the third floor. Who knew how many books and ledgers and scrolls were up there? Dozens or hundreds, maybe more.

The only way to find out was to get up there and get started.

I rested my Faytling on my chest and moved to the wrought-iron staircase that spiraled up to the second level. At the blue velvet drapes that cordoned off the Sanctum, I paused. My thoughts drifted to the divining pool on the other side and another idea took hold.

Since I was here to prove Krol wrong, would it be just as easy to catch him in a lie as it would be to search aimlessly through stacks of records? It would probably take less time.

There was, however, the rule against Converging without a witness.

But what if…?

No, I pushed the notion from my mind and hurried up the staircase. The image of Mr. Bailey at the Windsor divining pool still burned in my memory. The crimson mist spilling over the pool's rim. The reek of malice in the air. He'd betrayed Druansha, and the Fayte Order, and everything they stood for. *We* stood for. I couldn't repeat that mistake, even if I had better intentions.

I had to focus on what I'd come here to do.

When I reached the third level, it appeared as tidy as the second. There were no piles or stacks or any of the mess I'd envisioned after Clara's description. Maybe this wouldn't be as bad as I thought.

I went to the first panel and pressed the plaque to release the bookshelves. When I pulled it across the floor, my heart sank. Ragged scrolls, dusty leather volumes, and assorted journals were stacked and piled and pushed together with no semblance of order at all. I found the same behind the second panel and the third and the fourth.

I stepped back, stunned by the disorganization. The archivist hadn't made little progress before she was dismissed, it was clear she'd made none at all.

But I had to start somewhere.

On the first shelf, a large, brown leather journal sitting unsteadily atop three scrolls caught my eye. Its front cover read *The Recorded Events of the Addington Family* in golden script. I opened to a page titled "Births" in handwritten letters with rows of entries dating back to the seventeenth century. So many names and dates alongside symbols I didn't understand. I flipped to another page marked "Weddings," which had similar rows of names and dates and locales, and still more symbols that made no sense. I closed the book and returned it to the shelf, standing it upright and making a place for it at the beginning of the shelf.

Another, thinner volume read *Addendum to the Council Codex*. I pushed it up against the first.

A third, the largest of the three and older, if the tattered edges of its pages were any indication, had no title at all. I pulled it down and opened to the first page, where I found an inked illustration of a pale young woman in ancient Gaelic dress shaded purple and blue with accents of silver and gold leaf. In flourishing script, the title read simply *The Collected Writings of Eithne, Daughter of Boudica, First of the Fayte Guardians.*

Beneath my gloves, my fingers tingled.

Mrs. Crossey had told me the great warrior queen became the first Fayte Guardian when Druansha imbued her with new powers and strength to aid the fight against the Roman invasion. In the end, it hadn't been enough to defeat the usurpers, but those powers had persisted and were passed on to Boudica's daughters through a blood ceremony before the ancient queen died. The sisters, according to legend, were changed by the blood as well and had continued their mother's mission to guard their homeland and passed that legacy on to their descendants. That was the origin of the Order, according to Mrs. Crossey, but now, I held that history—our history—in my own hands.

Only what she would have you know of it.

The words caught me by surprise. I willed myself not to panic. "How did you know I was here?" I whispered, knowing he could hear me, wherever he was.

The stone shows me.

I pulled the Faytling from beneath my collar and stared at it. The crystal had betrayed me. But how?

It does not betray. It connects.

As the sibilance of his words echoed in my ear, I returned the book to the shelf and fought the urge to run down the stairs and back to the safety of my room.

You cannot run. I am wherever you are.

"I want you to leave me alone!" My control was slipping, but I couldn't help it.

You want answers. I can provide them.

"I don't believe you."

Something rumbled like laughter.

What do you fear, my child?

"Get away from me!" I closed my eyes and covered my ears, the leather of my gloves cold against my skin. I shook my head, willing him to leave. "Go away!"

I rushed to the stairs, but something caught my eye in a mirror. I saw not just myself and the room reflected back at me, but there was an image I recalled all too well from the Gray Woods. The powerful legs clad in black trousers and boots to the knee. A black vest over a muscular torso mottled and gray like a graveyard stone. The long black hair smoothed back from red serpentine eyes.

My mind told me to run. I *wanted* to run and never look back.

Why? I have so much to show you. So much…

"I don't want it." Tears welled, but I forced them back. I wouldn't give in to them. They did no good.

Yes, you are strong like...

He was still there. Those crimson reptilian eyes trained on me from within that mirror. The weight of that malevolent glare made me turn away. "I'm not like you. I never will be."

That rumbling, grumbling laughter again. Then it paused.

Not like me. Like your mother.

My breath stopped. Everything stopped.

"You know nothing of my mother," I lashed back.

Don't I?

How dare he mention her. How dare he pretend. The fear left me, leaving raw anger in its place.

Yes, the anger is good. I can tell you more than anything on these shelves. They won't tell you what you need to know. They'll never tell you. Come to the water.

"What do you know about her?"

I was still angry. Furious, even. But if he could tell me anything about my mother, wouldn't it be better than searching blindly through these shelves? I didn't even know what I was looking for.

Let me show you.

I told myself I had no choice.

At the edge of the divining pool, I removed my gloves and dipped my fingers despite my fear. I hated myself even as I did it, but I couldn't resist.

At once, my Faytling glowed a bright white light.

Call my name.

"Krol." The name tasted bitter on my tongue.

The water turned a deep crimson, and a billowing mist rose from its surface. I knew there was no turning back.

Good. Very good. Tell me what you want to know.

My breath quickened, and my mouth went dry. I swallowed hard. "Tell me my mother's name."

Madeleine. Her name is Madeleine Ross.

Ross? Had I heard that surname before? I couldn't recall. But could I believe him? This could all be a lie.

It is no lie.

I closed my eyes and cringed. It was true. He knew every thought.

"Where is she now? Where is Madeleine Ross?"

Silence.

"You don't know?"

Again, nothing.

I swayed my fingers through the water. "Are you still there?"

I am.

But his voice sounded smaller, more distant.

I have not thought of Madeleine in a long time.

A knot formed in my chest. A longing. Of course, I longed for my mother, but this was different. This wasn't *my* emotion. It was his.

"Is she alive?"

More silence. I was about to give up when I heard, faintly:

She endures.

Those words struck me like punch to the gut. My mother was alive!

"Where is she?"

Another time. Another day.

His voice drifted away. The crimson faded from the mist, and the water again turned clear. Everything returned to how it had been, and I knew he was gone.

The secrets he had yet to tell me would have to wait.

CHAPTER EIGHT

MADELEINE ROSS. I tightened my grip on the divining pool's edge and repeated the name, letting the syllables reverberate within me. Did they stir old memories? Did they ring of truth?

Was this finally the answer to my forgotten past?

And there had been that tantalizing promise: *She endures.*

It was more than I had ever dreamed.

Unless it was too good to be true...

I stood there, waiting for something inside to click, something to latch into place and open a door. Shouldn't her name have sparked an epiphany?

There was nothing.

A quiet voice, perhaps the voice of reason or just my doubts, whispered, *He gave you a name, but it could be anybody's name. It might not be your mother.*

Doubts were getting the better of me again.

I pushed through the Sanctum curtains and found the grandfather clock. It was nearly midnight. I should get back to my room. Marlie was probably waiting up.

But who was I kidding? I couldn't sleep. Krol had given me a name, but it meant nothing if it was a lie. I had to know who Madeleine Ross was, and the only way to do that was *up there*. From the main level, I could see only the wrought-iron railing and the shadow of the rooms above.

If Madeleine Ross was my mother's name and if she was a Fayte Guardian, as Mrs. Crossey insisted, she would be recorded somewhere in those volumes.

It was the only incentive I needed. I scurried up to the third level and pulled out one shelf and then another, searching for something—anything—relating to the Ross family. I pushed aside a volume for the Cathers, and one for the Grangers and the Hills. Then the Kebleys, the Lloyds, and the Crosseys.

The Crosseys?

I couldn't resist. I muscled down the rather large black book, sending a constellation of dust motes dancing through the air. I blew away the thin layer of dust before cracking it open. The contents were entirely handwritten. I landed first on a page titled "Births." I flipped again and landed on "Deaths." I thumbed through until I found the marriages. I scanned each neatly written entry, searching for a possible year. Sometime in the early 1800s. Then, there it was, on May the third, 1823. "Sylvia Trindle married to Vincent Crossey."

Mrs. Crossey's husband's name was Vincent. I considered what he must have been like, what kind of man he had been, but then I thought of her. In 1823, she would have been so young, maybe younger than I was now. She wouldn't have been Windsor Fayte's Master Scryer yet. That would come later.

So, a wedding would have been everything to her. A new bride beginning her family. Then it struck me: she'd never mentioned him or told me if she was a mother. I'd never even thought to ask.

I flipped back to the births and scanned all the entries after 1823.

Nothing.

I flipped more pages, looking for other clues and landed on the registry of deaths. My eye skittered across the page until it found the name. Vincent. The entry was dated November 1825. "Vincent Crossey killed by fever. Survived by a widow." No children.

In less than two years, her husband and that promise of a family had been taken from her. What sadness she must have endured, and it pained me to remember how much I'd railed against her. I should have known it would take someone who had experienced her own overwhelming pain to feel sympathy for mine.

I made a mental note to tell her how much I appreciated her the next time I saw her as I tucked the volume back on the shelf, arranging it among the other family volumes and sorting them into alphabetical order.

The sorting and arranging continued until, tucked beneath two ragged scrolls, I spied a brown leather spine that read *Ross Family Collection*.

Aha!

I pulled it down and opened it, searching any entries dated between 1800 and 1840. I found a Reginald Ross, a groundskeeper, had received a commendation in 1801. A sickness had been registered a year before that, and consumption was mentioned. Another page showed an entry for a Gemma Ross, a maid, who had been promoted from the kitchen to the royal drawing room in 1802. Then nothing.

Nothing? For more than fifty years?

I turned back and noticed torn edges close to the spine. Pages had been ripped out. Four at least, maybe more.

I skimmed the rest of the pages but found only older notations. Frustrated, I shoved the book back on the shelf. For a long moment, I scoured the shelves looking for anything else bearing the Ross name. Nothing did.

I returned to the Ross volume and removed my gloves. Gently, I ran my fingertips along the cover and waited for a vision. A swirling sensation set in that nearly knocked me off my feet. It indicated a ward on the book, but why?

Not that it mattered. I was no better off than before.

Madeleine Ross might be my mother, or she might be a stranger. So far, I had no evidence she existed at all.

When I finally did return to my room, all I wanted to do was crawl into bed and forget everything. I wanted to shove it all behind me.

Except I couldn't. Part of me was clinging to the hope that I'd discovered my mother's name.

A small voice whispered in my ear again: *You cannot accept one truth without the other.*

As I lie in the darkness, I realized I could no longer deny it.

I had to admit Krol could be my father, after all.

~ ~ ~

Krol's words must have replayed in my mind a thousand times as I tossed and turned in my bed, trying but failing to sleep. I'd been so eager to learn my mother's name, and maybe I had, but there were still so many other unanswered questions: What did she look like? What kind of person was she? Why did she abandon me?

That last one burned most of all.

Sometime in the middle of the long night, another idea came to me. Even if the old records wouldn't give me the answers I wanted, there might still be others who could. People who'd spent their entire lives in the Fayte Order would surely have heard of a Madeleine Ross.

At dawn, I was up and ready for the kitchen in record time. I reported early and was happy to see Clara already there. She put me to work on biscuits, and at first I did my best to focus on the task.

My plan was to keep my question to myself at least until noon, so it wouldn't raise suspicion. But by nine, as I was mixing a second batch of dough and Clara was cutting carrots, I gave in to my impatience.

"Have you ever heard of a maid named Madeleine Ross?" I kept my gaze locked on my flour-crusted gloves. I hoped the question sounded as casual as any of the other conversations we'd had across the table.

Clara held a carrot and sliced through it with a quick *tap-tap-tap* motion, leaving a trail of slender orange coins. She stopped and quirked an eyebrow. "Why would you ask such a thing?"

My fingers froze in place. "Did I say something wrong?"

"Aunt Maddie has been gone for years."

Aunt Maddie? My fingers remained locked in the dough. "I'm sorry. I had no idea. You're a Bellington."

"My mother is a Ross. Lavinia Ross, before she married my father. But you must already know that."

"I didn't," I stammered before mastering my composure. "I... someone mentioned a Madeleine Ross who'd been a maid in royal service years ago."

Clara's knife stopped mid-slice. "Someone was talking about Aunt Maddie?" Her usually bright expression clouded. "She worked at Buckingham Palace, with my mother, then Windsor right before she left."

"Left? Where'd she go? Do you know?" I tried to rein in my enthusiasm.

"We haven't seen her in ages. Who was talking about her? Have they heard something?"

Her eyes went wide with hope, and it broke my heart to shake my head. "No, it was nothing like that."

The dough became the sole focus of my attention. The heels of my palms pressed into the mound, pushing it and stretching it before I doubled it over on itself and repeated the motions.

We were quiet for a long time, and I hoped her attention had moved elsewhere, but then she whispered,

"Does Aunt Maddie have something to do with your research?"

The question paralyzed me, and I'd never been gladder that I'd never disclosed exactly what I was looking for in the Fayte records. I didn't want to tell her what Krol had told me, because then I'd have to explain all of it, maybe even about Krol himself. I wasn't ready for that. I had to say something, though, because she was watching me like she expected an answer.

I offered the only one I could muster: a shrug with half a smile. "Maybe? But probably not." I went back to the biscuits.

She wiped her forehead with the back of her forearm and scraped the cut carrots into a bowl. "If you ever do hear anything about my aunt, I hope you'll tell me. I'd very much like to know what happened to her."

I kept my eyes cast down. "Yes, of course."

For the rest of the day, I regretted saying anything because Clara didn't speak to me again unless it was necessary, and I did my best not to put my foot in my mouth again. I made my biscuits and cleaned up after myself. I even delivered the finished trays to the ovens without calling for a kitchen page for help.

When Clara finally released me for the evening, I was happy to get away. I gulped down a small bowl of stew in the dining hall and hurried to my room.

Since Marlie wasn't there, I pulled out my memory box so I could practice. I couldn't make myself open the lid, though. I didn't want to slip into someone else's memories. More than ever, I wanted to know what happened to my own, and I wanted to know if Madeleine Ross was part of them.

~ ~ ~

Marlie was already gone by the time I awoke the next

morning, but there was a small linen-wrapped bundle on the dresser with a note. *For you,* it read in her curlicue script. The smell told me what the package contained even before I opened it.

Basil.

Whether she'd given me some of her own or collected more, I didn't know, but I was grateful either way. I slipped the offering into my pocket and hurried to the kitchen.

Later, while a batch of biscuits was in the oven, I pulled out the packet to test my theory. After plucking the fragrant leaves from the stems and stacking them atop each other, I cut the stack into slender ribbons before tucking them between a smooth layer of butter and thinly sliced cucumber.

"I didn't know you were making the tea sandwiches today," Clara said when she noticed what I was doing.

She'd been so pleasant all morning, I resolved to keep any future questions about Madeleine Ross to myself.

"These aren't for the staff," I said. "It was an idea I wanted to try out. What do you think?" I handed her one of the small morsels and watched her take a bite.

"Cucumber and butter, and what else? Is that basil?"

When she smiled, I released the breath I'd been holding. "It is. Do you like it? I wanted to do something different, like you said."

She lifted the top slice of bread and examined what was beneath. "It's lovely. Not overpowering, but a light note against the creamy butter and the crisp cucumber. How many did you make?" She peered over my shoulder.

"Only one. Do you think I should change anything? I was considering radish slices."

She shook her head. "Too bitter. But this is delicious. Just cucumber, butter, and basil. Nothing else?"

"A few grains of salt. Maybe I could make a batch for the Servants' Hall table for tea?"

She cut me a look. "No, let's stick with a pan loaf and butter for today."

My hopes sank. If she didn't think the sandwiches were good enough for our colleagues, they certainly weren't good enough for the Queen. I squared my shoulders to hide my disappointment. "Of course. I'll get started on the bread."

As I gathered the ingredients, I wondered if she'd assigned me a pan loaf because it was the easiest to make. I wadded up the remaining basil stems and threw them into the nearest bin, along with what was left of the cucumber.

Frustration simmered in my gut while I worked, but by the time I was kneading the dough on the worktable, it had reduced to dull resignation. Clara had probably done me a favor. If my experiment had failed, at least it was a secret between the two of us.

Imagine how it would feel to walk into the dining hall and see a platter of half-eaten sandwiches or to overhear complaints whispered behind my back. Her honesty might have been harsh, but at least she'd spared me something worse.

Instead of the tea sandwiches, I focused on the pan loaf, sticking strictly to the recipe and not deviating in the least. I melted butter and drizzled it over the top then dragged a knife's tip across the length before taking it to the ovens.

As I lingered, watching the attendants work, Lucas entered the kitchen with his attention directed to my usual worktable. Was he searching for me? Despite myself, my hopes rose, and I nearly called out. Before I could, the door swung open again and Ivy appeared. She hurried to catch up to him and grabbed him by the elbow, pulling his attention back to herself.

When he held the Servants' Hall door for her, I could feel my heart shrivel in my chest. I knew I had no right to be upset. He'd never promised me anything, and those long talks of ours… well, that's all they'd been. Pointless words and, for me, silly wishful thinking. Perhaps it could have been more if he weren't attached, but he was. Nothing I could do would change that.

That thought turned itself over in my mind as I watched the oven's heat work its magic on the loaves. When they were toasty brown, a young man shoved a flat wooden paddle beneath them and pulled them from the flames. I set them out to cool and spent the rest of my evening preparing a new batch of clotted cream for the next morning's scones. It was mindless work, and for that I was grateful. I didn't want to think, not about Lucas or Ivy or anything. I wanted to be numb.

CHAPTER NINE

LONG AFTER NIGHTFALL, when I was sure the kitchen would be clear, I grabbed my coat from the peg beside the door.

"Off to the pantry," I said in case Marlie was only pretending to sleep.

"Hmmm-mmm," she murmured and rolled over.

I hurried through the kitchen's shadows and carefully made my way to the secret passage and the tunnel below. Though I had permission, my heart raced, and I jumped at every sound. It was the possibility of encountering that other presence that had me on edge.

I resisted the urge to touch my Faytling. I'd grown used to holding it for comfort and reassurance, but that was out of the question now. It connected us, he'd said. Whether it was true or not, I didn't know, but I wasn't willing to test the fact, either. I would have left it behind if it wasn't required to unlock the door.

When I reached Fayte Hall, I pulled it from my neck, completed the task as quickly as possible, and returned it to its hiding place, hoping I hadn't alerted Krol.

Tonight, I wanted to be left alone.

I moved quickly yet quietly up the spiral staircases until

I was back among the disorganized library. When I pulled out the first bookcase, I found the pile of ledgers, journals, and scrolls just as I'd left them.

Only this time, I planned to expand my search. Since I'd failed to find anything useful among the Ross family history, I decided to look for anything pertaining to the Fayte Guardians of Buckingham Palace, Lavinia Bellington, or anything that might relate to Madeleine Ross.

As I skimmed the volumes, the Fayte Heir's memoir once again caught my eye. My fingertips lingered on it. As tempting as it was to delve into that history, though, I needed to focus on Madeleine.

But where to begin?

After two hours, I'd scoured through all five bookcases and found nothing more about the Ross family in general and nothing at all about a Madeleine Ross specifically.

Somehow, I must have missed something. I wandered the rows again, scrutinizing each volume more closely. One whole shelf contained nothing but scrolls and tattered ledgers, with newer leather tomes shoved along the bottom shelf. I pulled one of the newer ones. The cover read *Converging Notes, Year 1792 to 1794*. The volumes alongside it included a range of years culminating with 1805. I grabbed one and opened it.

"Should His Majesty travel to the north during the spring, there is grave potential for malicious intent. Beware of poisoned food and drink offered to him from unknown sources before the next moon. Revealed the Nineteenth of March in the year 1787."

I flipped forward.

"Before the next moon, Her Highness Princess Amelia will suffer great pains of the limb and all care should be taken to maneuver her to the house in Worthing, where she will receive proper care. Revealed the Sixteenth of April in the year 1798."

These pages were all filled with the Lady's warnings, hundreds of them, if not thousands, but there was little chance anything here would pertain to Madeleine Ross.

I shoved the volumes back, arranging them into a tidy and chronological order, and moved to the next bookcase.

There, on a nearly empty shelf, sat a messy pile of old papers and on top of them a brown leather book that appeared newer than the others. I heaved it from its place. The cover read *Historical Record of the Balmoral Order of the Fayte*.

Now, this might be useful. Surely there had to be something about Clara's family in it, and if so, maybe something about Madeleine as well. I cracked it open to its beginning pages.

I took a seat on the nearest couch, lit a candle on the adjacent table, and turned to the opening page.

The first Fayte Guardians to be dispatched to the Scottish Highlands to serve at the new Balmoral Castle arrived primarily from Windsor Castle, with others from Buckingham Palace and elsewhere. They arrived with the singular purpose of creating the foundation for Fayte service and protection for the royal family in this new environment and neighboring regions.

The Lady of the Fayte had foreseen that a new Sanctum would be required even before the property's deed was transferred and the royal plans were known, so preparations were well underway by the time construction began on the new castle. During Scryer Lavinia Bellington's Convergences—

Convergences? How had they conducted ceremonies before the new hall was built? What did they use for a divining pool? I made a mental note to ask Clara, then continued—

During Scryer Lavinia Bellington's Convergences, the Lady revealed a system of interconnecting caves in the forest beyond the castle grounds that would provide a formidable home for a new Fayte Hall.

As a High Councilor had not yet been named for the region, the information was shared with Guardian Elder James Starwyck. Long known for his talent with woodworking and masonry, Mr. Starwyck assumed the task of overseeing the construction with the help of his son, James Lucas Starwyck.

Work on the structure stalled in the early stages of the effort, but once construction on the new castle began in earnest, it became easier to hide the procurement of materials within the budgets and deliveries for the new castle. Any questions about cost overages and missing shipments were explained as the result of miscounts or mismanagement.

The work itself was carried out largely under the cloak of darkness as Fayte Guardians and their team of hired carpenters and masons worked throughout the night, protected from the curious eyes of neighboring villagers by the careful application of wards.

Upon occasion, ramblers and highwaymen happened upon a work site. In those instances, the intruders would be welcomed as friends and invited for cups. In the morning, they would awaken on the side of a road with a roaring headache and lost memories. Inevitably, they attributed any incomprehensible visions to too much drink or the work of fae folk. No questions or suspicions ever came of it or hindered the Fayte effort.

Under the Starwycks' supervision, work progressed swiftly. Together, they oversaw the laying of every brick and the set of every stone and plank.

I skipped forward to find the author elaborated at length on the grandeur of the air apparatus and many other innovations, while recounting almost nothing about the Fayte Guardians themselves.

I placed the book back on the shelf then sank into the nearest chair to rethink my plan. There had to be some other way to get the information I sought.

There is, and you already know where to find it.

I sighed. I'd been waiting for him to speak. I'd felt him lingering at the back of my thoughts since I'd picked up the history book, but he'd kept his silence.

Are you ready?

I glanced back at the chaos of so many books and scrolls piled onto the shelves. Even if the answers to my questions were there, how many nights would I waste searching for them?

Come to the water.

I didn't trust him, not in the slightest, but maybe I didn't have to. If he revealed more, it could aid my search, or it could prove he was lying. At this point, either was preferable to this blind pursuit.

By the time I'd made up my mind, I was already down the stairs and standing at the blue curtain. Inside, the divining pool's glow had brightened, making the swirls and veins in the alabaster stone more defined. A soft, cloudy mist rose from the surface and rolled over the rim before falling to the polished stone floor. I hesitated.

Yes, it could be a trap, but I wasn't getting anywhere on my own. Wasn't it better to try?

Slowly, I removed my gloves and lowered my fingers into the basin. The moment my skin touched the water, the mist turned a deep crimson.

Welcome back.

The air around me went cold.

"Where are you?"

We are together.

My chest tightened. Fear gripped me, but something else, too. Something that kept me in thrall.

We are alike, you and I.

That thought sliced through me. Flashes returned of what he'd done back at Windsor. The people he'd hurt. The innocent farm girl he'd killed. "I'm not like you."

But you are.

No, I wouldn't let him convince me of that. I straightened to my full height and raised my chin. "Tell me something about my mother."

You want to know if what I've already told you is true.

"Yes, I do."

I have told you the truth.

"You told me a name."

Is that not enough?

"It could be a stranger's name. I want to know more."

Then you will see it now.

Before I could ask what he meant, the disorienting feeling of a vision came over me. When the blurring stilled, a woodland scene emerged. The warmth of a summer evening enveloped me, and a young woman, perhaps twenty, with long, dark hair pulled back into a knot, was sitting beside a secluded stream with an elaborate silver goblet adorned with rose-colored crystals. I'd seen that goblet before, and it took only a moment to realize it was the one I'd seen encased in glass in Fayte Hall.

But what was this woman doing with Boudica's chalice beside what appeared to be one of the small streams that flowed around Windsor Castle?

This is your mother. This is Madeleine.

Of course, it was. My questions about the chalice fell away. This was my mother. It had to be because now that I could see her clearly, it was like looking into a mirror. She had my fair skin and blue eyes, my narrow shoulders and slender waist. More than that, though, she had that strange intensity I sometimes noticed in my own expression.

With growing wonder, I watched the young woman fill the chalice with water from the shore and submerge her fingertips like a Scryer.

She would sneak out with that old cup to practice among the oaks. She thought she was alone, but I was there as well, watching.

"You didn't speak to her?" I whispered as though the woman in the vision might overhear.

Watch.

As soon as he said it, the young woman interrupted her incantation to sob. "Why don't you answer, Lady? What am I doing wrong?"

The young woman's tears dripped into the cup, and

they mingled with the water from the stream. Behind her and unseen by her, thick fog crept through the trees, obscuring the ground and inching closer to her.

Then I saw him. A man standing at the edge of the mist. Tall and powerfully built, he was dressed in a woodsman's trousers and simple jerkin, but the black fabric was spun of such fine thread, it seemed to cast a sheen. His silky dark hair was pulled back from the hard lines of his face and captured by a thin leather strap that hung down the middle of his back. His bare hands hung at his sides, and upon his forefinger, a single black metal band set with a crimson stone.

I knew that ring, and in that instant, I knew the man was Krol, though he was so different. His eyes were not serpentine red but a chocolaty brown and amiable as they gazed upon my mother.

When he took a step, a twig broke beneath his foot, and the woman turned, startled.

Don't be frightened.

His words seeped into her mind without speech, just as they did with me, yet I was aware of them.

She tensed. "You speak as the Lady of the Fayte speaks. Who are you?"

One touched by your sadness. What vexes you?

There was such kindness in that voice, I hardly recognized it. Where was the anger and sarcasm I knew?

The woman swallowed her emotion and rubbed away her tears. "I don't belong here. I miss my family. I've been sent here to be trained, but I don't want it. I want to go home."

You are lonely. Surely, you have friends.

"There's no time for friends. I only work in the kitchen or work at this." She stared into the chalice, and I could feel the weight on her heart. "I hate it."

But to be a Fayte Guardian is to be special, is it not?

Her eyes shot up. "You know of the Guardians?"

I do. The rigid line of the man's deep pink lips softened with a smile.

His admission put the woman at ease. "I don't want to be special," she confided, and by then her tears had dried. She glanced up at the sky to see night was falling. "I've been here too long. I should return to the castle."

There was reluctance in her voice, and perhaps that's what made Krol bold because he asked, *What is your name?*

"It's Madeleine."

A beautiful name for a beautiful woman.

Her gaze dipped, and she blushed.

Will you return tomorrow, Madeleine?

A coy smile touched her lips. "Will you be here?"

He nodded, and her first promise was made.

The scene faded, and I was again aware I was standing in the Sanctum, alone with my fingers in the crimson mist of the divining pool.

When my wits returned to me, I said to Krol, "That was the beginning?"

It was.

"What happened next?"

This is enough for now.

Enough? Now that I could feel the connection, I couldn't be satisfied with so little. "You said she's alive. Where is she?"

You will know that in time. You must do something for me first.

I didn't want to barter. But what choice did I have? "What do you want?"

Imagine a great ball of crimson light. Imagine that light all around you.

What an odd request. "Why?"

It protects you from prying minds.

Fayte Guardians had that ability?

I'd only thought the question, but he answered.

Doubtful. They have grown too weak and forgotten the old ways. They are not true Fayte Guardians any longer. They pretend to be strong like the old ones, but they have no power. The light will protect you from my sister. Until we can set things right.

Guilt struck me. Wasn't I already hiding my thoughts from her? "Why must I do this?"

I already knew the answer. At least, I thought I did. Druansha despised Krol. If she discovered I was communicating with him, she'd know I'd betrayed her and she'd despise me, too, if she didn't already. She had tried to banish him from this world. I could only imagine what she would do to me.

So, I imagined myself within that ball of red light. It was only a protection spell, he told me.

You are strong because my blood flows through you. Far stronger than the others.

Was I? My fingers and arms tingled at the thought of it. I certainly was stronger than Marlie and Mrs. Crossey. Stronger than any of them. He'd said the Fayte were weak, and perhaps he was right. What could they do without Druansha's help? They only carried out her bidding.

A smoldering rage seeped through me. I'd never been angry at her before, but I understood how Krol must have felt. His anger was becoming my own. His frustration and betrayal flowed through me.

Somewhere in the ether, I could feel my father's approval. I could feel him beside me.

Together we will take what is ours. Yes. You feel it now.

I don't know how long I stayed there, wrapped in that crimson mist, but when his presence receded, when I knew he was gone, the rage remained. And that's when I finally understood.

I was my father's daughter.

CHAPTER TEN

THE NEXT MORNING, I entered the kitchen to find Clara peeling potatoes. "You're late," she said, her voice unusually somber.

"Am I?" I knew I should be sheepish, but I wasn't. It was difficult even to pretend otherwise. "I got here as quickly as I could."

Perhaps that was true, considering I really wasn't trying. What could she do to me, after all? I'd spent the night replaying the scene Krol had showed me of my mother. Was it the proof I'd sought? It was difficult to focus on anything else, especially anything as mundane as making biscuits or pan loaves or whatever brainless task she'd assign me today.

I couldn't share any of that frustration with Clara, however.

Not that it mattered. Her attention had already turned, along with everyone else, to the head chef, who had moved to the center of the kitchen. "The Queen and the royal family are expected by month's end."

Behind me someone grumbled, "Already? It's too early in the season. It's not even summer yet."

The complaint must have come from someone who

wasn't a Guardian, for everyone in the Order had been expecting the visit.

"I heard it's because of that business with the East India Company," another whispered. "Now that Her Majesty has nationalized it, she's learning she can't be in two places at once. India is half a world away, for goodness' sake. It's taking a toll."

Clara was behind me at the worktable. I leaned back and whispered. "Is there anything special we need to do to prepare?"

When she didn't answer, I glanced back over my shoulder. Her head was down, and she was staring at something in her hand. When I peered around, I could see it was a tiny slip of paper. "What's that?"

She straightened and shoved the paper in her apron pocket. "Nothing." Her face colored a deep shade of pink before she grabbed a wooden spoon, dunked it in the tall copper pot, and stirred furiously.

"Clara, what's wrong?"

"Nothing at all. Everything is fine. It's just..." She sighed and pulled the wooden spoon from the stew and dropped it on the worktable, ignoring thick gravy that dribbled across the floor, leaving a trail of puddles between the pot and the table.

I was about to ask if she wanted help cleaning up the mess when she untied her apron and tossed it on the table. "Will you excuse me? Something has come up. I have to find my sister."

She was off and striding down the corridor before I could reply.

As I grabbed a rag to clean up the mess she'd left, I wondered what was so urgent that she had to dart off. When I bent to the floor to clean up the gravy, I saw a small curl of white paper nudged up against the stove. It was the paper Clara had been reading, and the one she'd tried to hide.

I glanced around to be sure no one else noticed it before I picked it up. Carefully, I unfurled the note. A single line of handwritten script read, "The trees are the answer. Have you told anyone else? Eager for reply!"

It was a strange note, to be sure, but why had it upset Clara? What were her and her sister hiding?

There was only one way to find out. After mopping up the mess, I went to the pantry, where no one could watch what I was about to do, and closed the door securely. I slipped off my gloves and retrieved the paper from my apron pocket. I gripped it tightly between the fingers of both hands.

Instantly, the topsy-turvy feeling of a vision came over me. When it subsided, I was in a small room of a simple cottage. A bluish-gray bird was sitting on a window ledge looking at me, its head tilting one way and then another. A quill was in my hand, fingers crooked and spotted with age, and it was moving swiftly across a slip of paper. This message was important, urgent even, I could feel it with every intense pen stroke. When a long lock of coarse silver hair fell over my shoulder and brushed the top of the desk, I didn't even pause to sweep it away.

"Are you Jane?"

The words yanked me from that other world back to my own. I clenched my eyes and willed my senses to settle back into normal working order. Then I took a deep breath and turned back toward the door to find a washing maid I'd seen but never spoken to before. I smiled. "I am."

The young woman smiled in return. "I thought so. I saw you made the clotted cream yesterday. Was there any left after yesterday's tea? We need it for today's service."

I tried to remain composed. She hadn't seen what I was doing, at least I didn't think so. "There was quite a bit left. I put the tub beside the butter crocks on the dairy shelf."

The girl grimaced. "You're sure that's where you put it?

Couldn't be anywhere else?"

"I'm sure. I asked Clara where it should go, and she said the shelf was the best place for it. Isn't it there?" There had been enough to last two more days, at least.

She shook her head. "We've searched everywhere. Why would someone take the clotted cream of all things?"

As she wandered back down the hall muttering about the kitchen thief striking again, I shoved my hand into my pocket and considered trying another vision.

But no, it was too risky. I slipped on my gloves and went back to work.

~ ~ ~

After midnight, I made my way back to Fayte Hall. I didn't waste time searching for anything useful among the bookshelves. I went directly to the divining pool, where I could feel Krol's presence even before I submerged my fingers. "Show me more," I whispered into the billowing mist that rose from the water's surface.

Instantly, the familiar swirling sensation came over me, and when it faded, I could see the clearing beside the river again. Madeleine was there with the chalice, breathless as though she'd been running and searching the veil of mist blanketing the ground. She was looking for him, I had no doubt.

"Are you here?" she called.

A breeze rustled the leaves, and a crow cawed in the distance.

Then a voice—his voice—answered. *I'm here. Fill the vessel.*

She did as he asked, lowering the cup's lip into the rushing stream. When she tilted it back up, he said, *Dip your fingertips and think of me.* She followed his instructions once again.

Thank you.

The words felt closer. She spun around to find him leaning against an oak, dressed just as before.

Don't be frightened.

The lyrical tenor of his voice put her at ease.

What happened next transpired like a dream. The two of them sat beside the burbling brook, talking of their families and their hopes, about everything and nothing, and it went on that way, day after day. Madeleine told him her absences had been noticed by her superiors in the castle, but she didn't care. Their scorn wouldn't stop her from seeing him.

You are not like anyone I've ever known.

His words came as they sat in silence, watching the stream.

"Surely, that's not true," she said, turning away and cheeks blushing. "I'm nothing special."

He stared at her for a long time then said, *You are very special, indeed. You know I'm not of this world, yet you have never asked anything of me. Why?*

"You have been a good friend. That's all that matters to me."

He'd been brushing his palm over the tall grasses but stopped, gazed into her deep blue eyes, and touched her knee. *Madeleine, I have never met anyone like you.*

The vision blurred and faded away.

"No, not yet. I want to see more."

The air. I must go.

His words drifted away, and I could feel him receding, too. The mist faded from crimson to gray then white before dispersing completely. It dispersed far faster than it did after a Converging Ceremony.

I heard it then, the soft, rhythmic chugging sound that filled Fayte Hall, even the Sanctum. The air apparatus was still hard at work while the castle slept. Mr. Starwyck had shut it down to Converge with Druansha but turned it back on when it was done.

Was that why Krol had to keep our Convergences short?

As I made my way back to my room, I wondered if anyone would notice if I shut it down? I knew how to get into the room, but then what? There'd been so many levers and switches and dials, I wouldn't even know where to begin.

If Lucas and I were on better terms, I might be able to find out from him. But the way things stood between us now, I couldn't imagine being in the same room with him, let alone ask him for a favor.

And who's fault was that?

Ivy Coombs.

Once again, I seethed at the thought of her. She'd already taken Lucas from me, and now she was keeping me from Krol.

~ ~ ~

Preparations for the royal visit meant cooks, maids, and pages occupied the kitchen day and night, effectively cutting off my access to the hall and to Krol, just when I needed him most.

He'd teased me with images of my mother, but there was still so much I wanted to know. What had happened between them, and where had she gone? He was holding back information, and I wanted to know what it was.

Even as my frustration festered, I couldn't share it with anyone, not even Druansha. Especially Druansha. Maybe that's why I couldn't shake the malaise that had settled over me. More than anything, I was missing my old friend, the dragonfly. Back before Madeleine Ross, Krol, and the Fayte Guardians, I could tell my dragonfly anything, and she was always the voice of reason.

Back then, she was my only friend.

Now that I supposedly had so many friends, I felt

lonelier than ever. Despite the happy smiles and eager invitations to share a corner of the Servants' Hall table and to laugh and chatter over the day's gossip and news, I knew I could never be honest with these people. Not really. If they knew my secret—that my father was an ancient and dangerous enemy to the Fayte Order and that I was betraying their trust by Converging with him in the Sanctum—their opinion of me would change. Even Marlie's, I had no doubt.

It would be only slightly better than Druansha's opinion, I suspected.

But deep down, I knew even that wasn't the reason for my foul mood.

If I was truly being honest, I would have to admit the truth about myself, which was that I was exactly what Krol was: a dark creature filled with malice and rage. I could feel his vengeful spirit within me, and I always had. It was why I never felt completely at ease with other people. I've always known I wasn't like them, and nothing I ever did would change that.

That thought gnawed through me like a parasite, and now not even Druansha escaped my scorn. In truth, she probably deserved it more than anyone. She had deceived me. Not only when she pretended to be my dragonfly friend, but when she withheld the truth from me. She had known my origins from the beginning. She knew my pain and confusion, and she never said a word.

She never even told me about my mother.

So, maybe being Krol's daughter wasn't the worst thing in the world. He was my family, after all, and at least now I knew where I belonged.

CHAPTER ELEVEN

MARLIE WAS SPENDING more time than usual on the upper floors, making them ready for the royal visit. So, I went to the Servants' Hall alone and tried to sit away from the others. It never lasted long. Strange to think how much I used to wish to be included in their idle banter because now I wanted none of it.

I was merely biding my time until I could return to the divining pool. I endured the table talk for as long as I could, but when Deirdre turned the subject to a complaint about the main drawing room's frigid temperature, which launched a spirited debate over the coldest room in the castle, I made my excuses and slipped away.

As was becoming all too common, there were still too many people in the kitchen to make my way to the pantry and Fayte Hall, so I took refuge outdoors, where I could at least take in the fresh air and pass the time.

Already darkness was creeping over the sky, painting the hillsides in dim twilight shades. The grounds appeared empty except for the usual guards, and they were easy enough to avoid.

Without a particular destination in mind, I wandered toward the area where the black rot had infected the trees to see if the decay had improved at all. It was easy to bypass the wards now that I knew about them by using my Faytling as a guide, but what I found didn't put my mind at ease. The black and gray patches that covered a few trees on my last visit now covered more than a dozen, maybe more. Some were blackened like a fire had consumed them, leaves and all. Others were gray and ashen, like something had drained them of life.

Krol was responsible. I didn't know how I knew it or how it could be possible, but I knew it in my bones. And I knew something else, too: It no longer upset me or made me angry as it had before.

Now, I knew it was part of his plan, and it left me feeling... nothing at all.

With my curiosity satisfied, I ventured deeper into the woods, along a trail directed toward the River Dee and Crathie. As daylight gave way to twilight, the forest's natural greens and browns darkened to charcoal grays and blues, making the valley feel even more isolated. Here, I felt so far away from everything, even time itself.

Was that what appealed to Queen Victoria? It was an amusing possibility, for who in her position wouldn't want an escape from the ceaseless duties of royal life? A place to call home without the responsibility of the past and the future hanging over her. To be not just a caretaker of a place—as she was at Windsor Castle and Buckingham Palace—but to have it truly feel her own.

As I walked, I wondered if she felt the grip of history, especially now that she knew about the Fayte Guardians. I wondered if it changed anything for her. Was she now more mindful of the servants in her midst?

Could that be why she was seeking refuge here out of season? Did she wish to escape the Fayte Guardians' attention at Windsor Castle?

Perhaps she didn't know we were all around her.

As I wandered up to the summit of Craig Gowan, a

shadow moved ahead, near the Purchase Cairn. My stomach turned to stone for even from a distance, I recognized that silhouette.

My instincts told me to turn back, but it was too late. He'd seen me, too.

"I wouldn't have expected to find you out here," he said when I approached.

"I'm allowed to go where I please."

He kicked at a twig in the grass in front of him. "Of course, you are."

I was being childish, lashing out over hurt feelings, and I hated myself for it. "I'm sorry," I said. "It's been a difficult day."

He turned back to the view over the valley below, and a sadness settled over him, more so than usual.

"You seem to have had one of those, too," I said.

He hunched and crossed his arms over his chest as though he were pulling into himself, making his long and lanky frame as small as possible. After a time, he said, "It's the anniversary of my mum's passing."

I could feel the pain of those words. Though he'd mentioned her death to me when we were at Windsor Castle, he hadn't elaborated. "I didn't know. When did it happen?"

He gazed up at the heavens. "It's been awhile. This was one of her favorite spots, though. It reminds me of her."

Whatever anger I felt toward him dissolved in that instant. He was hurting, and I would have comforted him if I could. But how? I'd never been good at those little gestures people offered one another, so I remained with my hands in my lap, limp as two dead fish.

I stared, as he did, into the distance. I searched for tender words to console him, but that had never been my strength, either. Instead, I stared at the woods around us. The gathering darkness was making it more difficult to see, but I could feel the trees and the stars beginning to twinkle between the clouds. "It's peaceful, isn't it? You can almost forget anything else exists."

"It is easy to forget," he whispered then turned to me. "But why would you need to forget anything? Things are going so well for you here. You're a hero because of Windsor. Everyone knows you saved the queen and brought back the Lady of the Fayte. You're all anyone can talk about. I know my father can't stop talking about you."

Something in his tone made it clear that touched a nerve.

"People have been kind," I said, measuring my words carefully. Should I tell him there were things that hadn't gone my way at all. No, I didn't trust myself. I couldn't tell him how surprised I was to learn about Ivy or to discover the fondness I thought we shared for each other had been nothing but a figment of my imagination. "But it hasn't been easy," I said finally.

"Easy? It seems it should be the easiest thing in the world. You have those." He pointed at my hands. Hands that could read the past and sometimes the present, if not yet the future. Hands that were my gift and my curse.

I stared at the ivory leather gloves that seemed to glow even as the light faded. "I do have these," I admitted, but what I couldn't tell him was they were still as much a burden as a gift. They'd allowed me to break Druansha's curse, but I'd still gladly give them up for ordinary hands. He probably wouldn't understand that, though. Better to change the subject. "What was your mother like?"

He turned back to the dimming horizon, and a sad smile crept across his face. "She was everything. Kind and smart. She taught me to read when I was four. She loved books. All kinds of books. But what she loved best was to sing. She sang while she worked around our cottage and when she cooked. I've never heard anyone with such a lovely voice. Sometimes when I'm out here, I can almost hear it in the wind."

A breeze rustled the leaves, and in the distance, a bird called out. I could swear I heard the River Dee splash and burble along its journey to Aberdeen and the sea beyond. It was nature's music, and floating above it, I imagined the whisper of a song.

"You must have loved her very much." He didn't know how lucky he was to have a mother who cared for him, who sang to him and loved him, even if it was only for a little while. I worked off a glove and touched his shoulder, running my bare finger along the seam.

He spun around, confused.

I pulled my hand back and covered it with the other. "I'm sorry. There was a leaf. I was brushing it away."

Of course, that wasn't it at all. I was hoping for a vision of that lovely memory. I coveted it despite myself, but that touch rendered nothing. I still didn't understand why he alone was immune to my visions. "What took her? Was it illness?"

He stared at the ground again and seemed to shrink away.

"No, nothing like that."

"Oh," I said, and nothing more.

We stood there for a long moment perched against the rocks, silent and still. I wrapped my arms around myself for warmth.

We stayed like that, not speaking. Just the two of us, alone with our thoughts, but together. It was comfortable, and I tried not to think of the kiss he'd nearly given me back at Windsor or the tender moments we'd shared along our journey. I dug the tips of my fingers into my palms, willing myself to forget.

"Do you want to know why my father hates me?"

I looked up at him, shaken out of my private agony. "I didn't know he did."

He chuckled, but there was no joy in it. "He does. And he has a right to. I've done something unforgivable."

I wanted to reach out and embrace him, to offer some semblance of comfort. But I didn't know how.

"I was the one who killed her. I killed my mother."

I stared at him, my mouth agape.

"I've never told anyone that before. I've never even said those words aloud. It's strange, actually."

"Why?"

He shrugged in a weary sort of way. "It's almost a relief to get it out. To finally admit what I did."

But he wasn't finished, and if he noticed my shock, he didn't show it.

"I've been hiding it all this time," he said.

"I'm sure you didn't…" I stopped myself. I had no right to say anything.

"It wasn't intentional, but it was my fault. She came looking for me when I should have been home. I was playing alone in the woods. It was so stupid." He scooped up a pebble and threw it. "I got caught up in a game I'd invented. Pretending there were ghoulies in the woods, and I was chasing them. They were only shadows, of course. But I should have been home, and I knew it. It makes no sense, even now. Why that day? Why didn't I go back when I heard her calling for me? She was with child, and it was nearly time. When my mother slipped and fell near the slope, she went into labor. The baby was born. Whether my sister arrived into this world dead or alive, no one will ever know because I was playing a stupid game. That's why he hates me, and I deserve it."

"I'm sorry." It was a completely inadequate thing to say, but I had no other words. No apology was going to bring her back, either of them, and nothing could lessen his pain.

Maybe that's what bonded us. Both of us knew the loss of a mother.

"Yes, I suppose that's it," he said.

He was still staring off into the distance, as if his

thoughts drifted out along the darkening horizon, as if completely unaware that he'd read my thoughts just as he had when we were leaving Windsor. I hadn't said anything then because Marlie had been with us and I was sure I'd sound like a fool for making such a wild accusation.

But this time, I was absolutely sure.

"What do you mean by that?" I asked plainly.

He gave me a funny look. "By what?"

"You said, 'I suppose that's it.' Why?"

He straightened. "You said that both of us knew the loss of a mother. I was agreeing with you. What's wrong with that?"

"What's wrong is that I didn't say it, I only thought it. How do you know what I'm thinking?"

His eyebrows furrowed. "I don't know. I could have sworn you said it. Are you sure?"

"Completely sure."

He clamped his lips together and shook his head. "I don't know what to say. I don't read minds."

I bit my tongue. If he didn't realize he'd done it at Windsor, I didn't want to tell him.

So instead we stood, each in our own thoughts, watching the nighttime sky claim what was left of the day.

When I looked at him again, he was looking back at me. Perhaps he'd been looking at me all along.

"I don't know why, but I feel at ease with you, Jane. I feel like I can talk to you." His hand, which had been perched beside mine against a rock, scooted closer and I felt his smallest finger nudge the edge of mine. Even through my glove, that touch tore through me like fire. I stared at our fingers, and when I looked up, our glances locked.

Something stirred in his eyes I hadn't seen before, not when we danced together at the Queen's masquerade ball, and not even when he almost kissed me in the moonlight later that night. There was something like passion or hunger, but it was more than that.

Then he turned away and stared into the distance again, off toward the small crescent of the moon.

Somehow, I knew he wasn't thinking of me any longer. His thoughts had turned to Ivy, the woman who would be his bride and share his life and hear his whispers in the moonlight.

The woman I hated more vehemently every day.

CHAPTER TWELVE

I **LEFT LUCAS** in the woods with an excuse that I was tired and ready to turn in for the night. I didn't care if he believed me, and he probably didn't. I couldn't sit there another moment pretending everything was fine or pretending he didn't belong to someone else.

All the anger and guilt that festered within me as I made my way back to the castle vanished, however, when I found the kitchen nearly empty. A night cook was on duty, but he was engrossed in the turning and basting of a massive shank over a low, smoldering fire.

He didn't even look up from his task as I hurried to the pantry door and slipped inside.

When I reached the divining pool and dipped my bare fingers into the water, I knew Krol was close.

I want to show you the world we can have. A world filled with warriors, not these weak and pathetic guardians.

I sensed his vengeance but pushed it away. "I want to see my mother."

There was a pause, and I wondered if I'd tried his patience. Then, *I will show you something better.*

At that, my inner sight clouded. When it cleared, he and I stood together in the Gray Woods, at the great tree where he'd hidden Druansha's crystal. A chill passed through me at the sight of it and of him. I'd grown used to the handsome stranger who appeared to my mother. But there was nothing of that aristocratic young man now, only the stony facsimile of a man with matted black hair, skin as gray and mottled as a tombstone, and those insidious red serpent eyes.

So, what was this? It wasn't another spirit flight, for I could feel the dampness in the air upon my skin, clammy and cold like I'd walked through a fog bank.

Krol pointed at something in the distance. The Gray Woods filled the landscape with its black and gray trees and dusty roan paths, but then there was something else. Swaths of green sparkled along the horizon. As we moved closer, I could make out hills, impossibly green hills punctuated by a vibrant rainbow of colors. Gemstones? No, they were flowers, extravagant blooms in every conceivable hue. Some stood as tall as the trees. But even more remarkable than the landscape was a crystalline structure with spires that pricked the sky. "What is that place?" I asked.

That is the Brightlands Palace. Go, see it for yourself.

I moved to the border between the Gray Woods and the other place. I had seen it before but only in glimpses. It had never looked real, but rather like a dream. Perhaps this was a dream as well, but I didn't think so. I stepped closer to the edge, to where the dead landscape ended and the verdant grass flourished. I stepped along the division like a tightrope dividing two lands. Krol stood beside me, watching me.

"Will you come with me?"

He shook his head, making his thin, straight hair brush across his shoulders. *Go and see our Queen. Tell her who you are.*

A queen? Here? But how would I find her?

The palace.

"Is my mother there?"

You will know that in time.

I didn't want to go, but the hope of finding my mother spurred me on. I stepped out of the gray and into the light, and the whole world changed. The dull emptiness of the Gray Woods gave way to a meadow that not only teemed with life but filled me in some inexplicable way with all its vibrancy. Standing on the lush blanket of grass, I could feel the color seeping into me. Not just the greens, but the reds and oranges and yellows of the flowers, and the blue of the sky. There were birds of indigo and purple, and butterflies and other flying things.

"This place is magic," I whispered.

This is where you belong. Your true home.

I heard his voice and sensed he was near, but I could no longer see him.

Tell them I wish to return, that we could return together.

His voice was different now. The arrogance was gone. As I walked, I tried to puzzle it out, but my attention moved to the palace. I could see more of it now. New spires appeared in the distance. Over the hill, they soared toward the heavens like shards of aquamarine glass and they called to me.

The farther I walked, the more I could see. Parapets and domes and buttresses.

Does it feel familiar?

His voice was clear, but I could no longer feel his presence. Was I imagining this? Was it a dream?

Not a dream.

Then the view of the crystalline palace faded, and I was again aware of the divining pool and my fingers submerged in the crimson water.

The abrupt change disoriented me. I wasn't ready to leave, so why had he pulled me away?

Or was it the machine again, ending our connection before its time?

No answer came from Krol, but I heard other voices. Men's voices. They were muddled, or perhaps I was groggy from the vision. Were they even from this world or the other?

Then I heard them again. They were here, near the Sanctum, I was sure of it.

I was glad I'd closed the curtains after I entered. I moved toward the hanging velvet to listen.

"He's already gone through half a pot of clotted cream and two jars of apricot chutney, not to mention half a dozen loaves of bread. Does he do anything down there but eat?"

Who were they talking about?

"You don't have to tell me," another, even gruffer voice said. "A scullery maid saw me walking off with a soda bread yesterday and nearly turned me in. Took some doing to convince her it was all a mistake."

"What'd you tell her?"

"Doesn't matter. I took care of it."

"Ah, c'mon. What'd you tell her?"

The other one hemmed and hawed and finally said, "Told her I was just trying to get her attention. That I liked the look of her."

Derisive laughter erupted from his companion before the other shushed him into silence. There was a heavy creaking sound. "Don't topple that there. You'll wake the guest."

"I don't think he ever sleeps. He's too busy eating."

They both laughed, but the sound slowly faded into silence.

I waited several heartbeats before peeking out. When I did, the gas lamps were still low, casting the hall in dim light. Where had the men gone?

I padded quickly to the main door to see if I could hear them in the tunnel. I listened but heard nothing. I checked the machine room, but they weren't there, either.

Were there other rooms Clara hadn't shown us? I searched the walls and had nearly completed the room's full perimeter when I heard the voices again, only muffled. I dropped to the floor and crawled behind a wingback chair. I held perfectly still, afraid I'd give myself away.

When the door unlatched, I bent to peek from beneath the chair to see if I could identify the men. I saw only the black boots and ivory trousers worn by the footmen. A clattering sounded like a food tray stacked with empty bowls and plates.

"He ate the whole roast beef. Who eats a whole roast beef in a day?"

"A wonder he can even walk after that. You took down tomorrow's requests, didn't you?"

"I got them. Couldn't trust you to remember, could I?"

"Oh, nice. Like I don't already haul around his dirty dishes and linens. What are you even here for, then?"

"To keep you in line, I suspect."

"I'll be glad when this is over and I can get a proper night's sleep."

"Quit your griping. It won't be much longer."

The main door creaked and swung open.

"I know, but I can't remember my last full night's sleep. Do you?"

"Who cares about sleep? There'll be plenty of time for sleep after the Queen's Slivering."

"*Shhh!* That's not to be said."

"What? It's not like anyone could hear us."

"How do you know?"

"No lights, no visitors. Yeah?"

"Fine, but you still shouldn't speak of it."

"Why? You getting cold feet?"

"Nah, I just want it done. I'm tired of waiting and pretending. I've never been good at pretending."

"True enough. Suppose that's why I get stuck with the job of nabbing his meals."

At the sound of the main door latching closed, I scooted to the edge of the chair and craned my neck around the side. Now that the coast was clear, I hurried to the corner and brushed my gloved fingers over the mahogany panels where the men had been standing.

I couldn't feel anything that felt like the edge of a door.

Somehow one was here, but how? I yanked off my gloves, tucked them into the waistband of my skirt, and tried again with my bare fingers.

A ridge protruded along a panel beside a potted silk palm, but even when I looked closely, I couldn't see it. The ridge seemed to form an outline of a door's frame, even though my eyes saw nothing of the kind.

With my fingers spread wide, I glided my hands over the surface, noting the rectangular shape. Where a doorknob should have been, there was a decorative molding block depicting a dragon curled around a bouquet of thistles in relief. Not unusual in a Scottish castle but oddly placed, nonetheless. I brushed my fingers over it. No levers. No knobs.

But...

I removed my Faytling and held it against the crest as I'd done at the main door. It fit over one of the long-stemmed thistles and notched into place. Instantly the stone glowed with a soft white light, and *pop!*—the wall moved. No, not the wall but a door activated by a spring. I pulled it back and peered around the side, where I could see a descending staircase.

"Hello?" I called down the narrow shaft.

"Who's there?" a harsh voice demanded.

It was too far away to identify, but I didn't plan on getting any closer. I pulled my Faytling back over my head and stumbled back, shutting the door closed behind me. I didn't hear the mysterious occupant coming after me, but I wasn't going to stick around, either. I raced to the main door and ran all the way back to the kitchen.

~ ~ ~

Krol stalked the crystalline hall like a caged tiger, making his crimson cloak swing wildly behind his black embroidered doublet.

"I refuse to do it, Mother." He glared at the throne glimmering like an opal beneath the palace's alabaster dome.

Upon it sat a woman of indeterminate years whose ghostly white hair swept back from a face as smooth and colorless as a pane of glass. She sat forward and watched Krol with a steady aquamarine gaze, saying nothing and her expression revealing even less.

"I told you, I will not do it," Krol continued, ignoring the liveried guards in their silver and blue uniforms standing along each of the four walls and the host of advisers and attendants who hovered about like so many flies.

The Queen shifted slightly, making the whisper-thin gown that hugged her womanly form shimmer from green to blue to violet. "You misunderstand, my son. I was not asking."

Krol halted, his pain plain upon his face. "Why would you ask such a thing? She has done you no harm."

The Queen's ivory forehead wrinkled for a shadow of a second. "You question me? Has she put these ideas into that beautiful head of yours?"

He couldn't reason with her, that was obvious. Instead, he opened his palms, appealing to whatever kindness or pity might still reside in that rock of a heart. "Mother, she has been a distraction, but one that will no longer keep me from my duties. I assure you."

A twitch of her lips gave him hope. She was listening. Perhaps she would retract the order.

"If that were true," she said, "you would have already done it."

He held his mother's glare, knowing that to look away would be interpreted as weakness. He knew what she wanted: a piece of Madeleine's soul. He'd been sent to the human world to collect it. Not from Madeleine, exactly, but from someone young. Someone healthy and robust. He'd done it countless times before, but when he'd come upon this woman, something had stopped him from entrancing her and placing his fingertip on her forehead to pull the phantom spirit from her physical form.

Perhaps if he'd just done it, instead of sitting with her and talking with her—what had possessed him to be so foolish!—Madeleine might not have noticed anything beyond a sense of weariness and malaise, if he'd kept the morsel small.

Perhaps that would have been enough to satisfy his mother.

But Krol knew his mother too well.

Once she drained that Sliver, she would want another. And if she developed a liking for it, she'd demand he pull it from Madeleine.

He never should have spoken to her. He certainly shouldn't have returned night after night. It was even worse than the little girl he'd befriended in those woods so many years before. The child had been so eager to hone her scrying skills that she'd welcomed his visits, at least until her meddlesome mother showed up.

He'd intended to reap from that girl's soul as a prize for his mother, but when the girl's mother had tried to banish him back to the Brightlands, he'd changed course. The woman was surprisingly strong for a human Scryer, but still no match for him, and it had been a good day for him when he presented his mother with the gift he'd ripped from that woman. The last he'd seen of the Fayte witch, she was nothing but a dried husk with little life left.

It still gave him a twinge of pleasure when he recalled it, but he couldn't do that to Madeleine. Not now.

"Have I lost you, as I lost your sister, to these ridiculous creatures? Perhaps I should send you both to the Gray Woods. Let you sit in that barren hole if you aren't grateful for what I provide."

His mother's reproach pulled him from his memories.

She continued, "Druansha is lost to me, I know that. She might amuse herself by meddling in the matters of that world, but I expect better from you."

"You have not lost me, Mother. I will not fail you."

It was what she wanted to hear, so it was easier to say it than argue. No one ever won an argument with Mother.

A smile lightened the darkness in her glistening eyes. "Of course I haven't. You are my heir. You know what is required."

102

CHAPTER THIRTEEN

CLARA CAME UP beside me at the worktable. "Are you going to slice that lemon or just stare at it?"

I tightened my grip on the fruit and lowered the knife tip to the rind. "I'm sorry. My mind must have drifted a little."

"A little?"

Instead of arguing, I sliced off six slender rounds. "What's next?"

She sighed and shook her head.

I'd obviously forgotten something important. But what?

"Sugar, eggs, and juice. Bring it all to a bubble on the stove, let it cool, then scoop it into the tart shell. The slices are for garnish."

Right. I was making a lemon tart.

I knew I needed to focus, but I'd hardly slept. Instead, I'd lain awake most of the night, puzzling over the reasons why Fayte Guardians would be delivering food so late to someone hiding in a secret room.

When sleep had finally come, I'd had fitful dreams of Krol. Strange dreams of him as he was in the visions with my mother, but he was in that crystalline palace. My mind had created a monstrous vision of the Brightlands Queen, and he'd called her Mother. It was a troubling possibility, even if it was only a dream. What was even more alarming was, in my dream, she'd ordered him to hurt my mother. I awoke with my night chemise soaked in sweat. I'd tried to tell myself it was only my mind playing tricks on me, but it didn't do any good.

As light washed away the darkness, I was already up and dressed and ready for the day, eager to put the nightmare behind me.

Clara arrived at the kitchen at our usual starting time and found me beside the stove, stirring the porridge pot.

"You're here bright and early," she said, as chipper as usual.

"Early, yes, but not so bright." I tried to stifle a yawn but gave up.

"Late night, then? Productive, I hope." She raised a single eyebrow.

I couldn't mention anything about Krol, but I wondered what she might know about the other matter.

"I'm not sure," I said. "I saw something strange." I knew I was taking a risk by mentioning it, but I told her about seeing the late delivery, keeping the location vague so as not to raise suspicion among anyone who might overhear.

"Maybe they were tending to the machine," she whispered curtly with a glare that made it clear I should not have mentioned Fayte business here, even obliquely. "It could be any number of things."

"But don't you think…"

The reproach in her eyes stopped me. "Right," I said. "Another time perhaps."

Sometime later, after the porridge was done and served and I'd finished the lemon tart, she must have known I was still bothered because she said, "If you're concerned about what you saw, you could always ask your friend, Lucas. It might have been him."

It wasn't Lucas. I would have recognized his voice. And after our talk on the hill, he was the last person I wanted to see.

After the dinner preparations were done, I intercepted Marlie on her way to the Servants' Hall.

"Let's get some air." I motioned toward the door.

"May I eat first?"

"Now would be better."

She hesitated. "Why? What happened?"

"Let's talk outside."

I was relieved when she followed me to the green lawn without any more questions.

She waited till I stopped then asked, "What's going on?"

"I went to the hall last night."

Her eyes widened. "Did you learn something?"

I didn't want to lie to her, so I ignored the question. "I saw two men taking food to someone who's staying down there. Did you know there's a hidden room?"

Her forehead creased. "How do you know it's hidden?"

"I found the secret door. When I opened it, someone called out. A man, but I didn't stay to find out who he was."

"Maybe he was working on the machine."

I slapped my forehead. Did Marlie and Clara both think I was dense? "It wasn't the machine room. There was a staircase leading down to a cellar, and the way the men talked, whoever is down there has been there awhile."

She bit her thumb. "Did you see who they were?"

I shook my head.

"Did they see you?"

"No. I hid till they left. Then I found the door and opened it with this." I tapped my Faytling beneath my blouse and apron. "It has a lock like the main door."

Her serious expression gave way to a wry smile. "Is this a joke?"

"What? Have I ever joked with you?"

Her smile vanished. "Good point. You're never funny."

"Marlie!" But that's as far as my protest went because even I knew she wasn't wrong. "They said something about a Slivering. Do you know what that is?"

"A what?"

"Slivering. It sounded like it was a ceremony."

"The Converging Ceremony isn't for another couple of weeks."

I'd considered that, too, but it didn't make sense unless they were trying to Converge with someone besides Druansha. Which is what I feared most because it would mean I wasn't the only reason Krol was here.

Marlie must have been thinking something just as ominous because the color drained from her face.

"We have to get help," she said in a low whisper.

Her fear fueled my own. "I know. But who can we trust?"

"Shouldn't we ask the Lady for help?" Marlie asked. "We could go to the Sanctum tonight. Both of us."

I froze.

"What's wrong? It'll be all right. You're initiated now."

"That's not it." Even though we wouldn't be breaking rules, as we had with Mrs. Crossey at Windsor, I didn't think I could hide that I was Converging with Krol from her. "I'm just not sure it's wise."

"Why?" Marlie frowned.

"Because…" My mind raced for an excuse.

"Because…?"

"Because the Lady didn't mention anything about it at the last ceremony. Don't you think that's odd?" I was grasping.

"Perhaps. But what difference does it make?"

"We're not Scryers. It probably wouldn't even work." I

knew it would, but I hoped Marlie didn't.

"What about Clara?" she asked. "Maybe she could persuade Ada to help us."

I wished we could go to Clara. I really did. "Clara would do it, but I'm not sure about Ada. She'd probably want to tell Mr. Starwyck, too. Besides, she doesn't like me."

"I'm sure that's not true." Yet even as she said the words, I could see she doubted them. "If we can't ask Clara, then it only leaves…" She gave me a look that told me she knew exactly who I was avoiding.

Lucas was the obvious choice. But I couldn't go to him. I wouldn't. Heat crept up from my collar to my cheeks just thinking about it.

"There has to be someone else."

She shrugged. "I can't think of anyone. Can you?"

I rubbed my eyes. She was right. He was the best choice, even if it pained me to admit it after that awkward conversation the night before. "Fine, but I don't even know where the wood shop is. Do you?"

I was hoping she wouldn't and that we could end this right here. Of course, I wasn't that lucky.

"It's near the conservatory. Behind it, near the gillie's shed."

The afternoon sky had darkened with the threat of rain, but the usual gardeners were still out, tending the flower beds and hedges. We passed a team of them as we made our way along the south lane toward the main road.

"Is that it?" Marlie pointed to a building set back from the conservatory. I'd noticed it before but took it for a barn.

As we neared, I heard hammering, and it was clear we were in the right place. I stuck my head through the open half of the Dutch door. Wooden chairs hung on pegs along the walls and from hooks in the rafters. Stacks of tables and cabinets were pushed into the corners, and each of the shop's four worktables was covered in sawdust and still more chairs and tables in some stage of repair.

The shop itself, however, appeared empty.

Marlie leaned closer to the dusty window, cupping her hands around her eyes to get a better view.

"I don't see him," I said. "Do you?"

She rubbed the side of her palm across the glass, trying to clear the layer of dust but only managed to smear it. "I can hardly see anything."

"Maybe I can help."

I didn't have to turn around to know it was Lucas who had come up behind us. I straightened and smoothed my apron before turning around. "We were looking for you, actually. Do you have a moment?"

He was dressed in overalls and a work shirt rolled to the elbows, with a brown cap pulled low over his eyes. He cradled a carved baluster stained a rich mahogany, and smudges along his fingers were nearly the same hue. "I have a few more of these to finish for the chapel and those chairs and tables there"—he nudged his chin in the direction of the worktables behind us. "But what do you need? Something break in the kitchen?"

"No, nothing like that." I glanced around to see if there were others around. Someone was leading a horse cart down the lane toward the road, but he wasn't close enough to overhear. Still, I lowered my voice. "May we go inside?"

He gave me a funny look and one eyebrow shot up. "So now you want to talk?"

I straightened and lifted my chin. If he was trying to make me uncomfortable, it wouldn't work. "If you wouldn't mind."

He shrugged, which infuriated me. He really didn't care, did he?

"Fine," he said. "Unless you plan to run off again."

Marlie looked from him to me and back at him. "Run off? What did I miss?"

When he looked away, I shook my head at her and mouthed, "Nothing."

She made a face that let me know she'd drop the subject for now, but we'd be discussing it later.

He moved alongside us, grabbed the door handle with his free hand, and held it open. "Ladies first."

Marlie stepped inside, and I followed. The air was thick with the crisp scent of cedar, oak, and pine, and it tickled my nose. I sniffed away a sneeze. "Is anyone else here?"

"It's just us. My father rode to Ballater to pick up a delivery. I don't expect him back till evening."

I believed him, but I glanced around anyway. It wasn't a large shop, half the size of the kitchen, maybe, and unless someone was hiding under a table, where it seemed mostly spare lumber and tools were stashed, there was no indication of anyone else. I stepped forward to see around a blind corner, where a small desk was nearly buried under stacks of loose papers and ledgers. A wooden cabinet butted up against a back door.

"Can you tell me what all the mystery is about?" he pressed. "You look worried. Has something happened?"

I wanted to be honest with him, but my anger was still getting the best of me. I bit my lip and debated whether I should just turn around and leave.

"Yes, something happened," Marlie interjected.

I glared at her.

She stood firm. "You have to tell him. How else are we going to find out?"

"Find out what?" He'd set down the baluster and was inching toward us. Toward me. "Are you in trouble?"

If he'd been angry, I might have fled back to the kitchen on the spot. But it wasn't anger on his face. It was concern. Perhaps even a hint of fear. It wasn't like him to exhibit such emotion.

"She saw something in the hall," Marlie blurted.

"*The* hall?" he asked.

She nodded, adding a knowing look.

"I can speak for myself, thank you." I was peeved but mostly because she was right. I needed the nudge, even if I didn't want it.

She held up her hands, palms out, and backed away. "Fine. Tell him the rest."

"Yes, tell me. What did you see?"

"I saw two men going into a hidden room. There was a staircase leading down to a cellar, but Clara has never heard of a lower room. I was wondering... I mean, *we* were wondering if you know what's down there."

"The machine room, is that what you mean?"

Did nobody believe I could tell the difference between the machine room and a cellar? "No. There's a door disguised by a panel beside the iron staircase. These men were taking food to someone, and they left with a tray of dirty plates. Someone is staying down there."

He looked at me like I'd lost my mind. "There's no one living in the hall and certainly not in a secret underground room. That's absurd."

Heat crept over my cheeks and ears. "I know how it sounds, but that's what happened. I thought you built that place. That's what Clara said. That's why we thought you would know."

"It was mostly my father's doing, to be honest. My father and the Elder Council. I know every part of it, however—the Library, the Sanctum, the Machine Room and the air apparatus, so you can believe me when I tell you there is nothing beneath that floor but ducts and channels to distribute the recirculated air."

"Might I interrupt?"

I stopped. We all did at the sound of Mr. Starwyck's voice from the small office around the corner. I moved to see him standing in the open doorway.

One thought seared through me: How much had he heard?

He closed the door behind him, latched it, and engaged the bolt lock before approaching us.

"Am I to understand that you saw this yourself? Two individuals opening a hidden door and descending to a secret cellar?"

As he neared, Lucas stepped back and kept his gaze on the ground. He wouldn't look at his father, and his father, I noticed, didn't look at him.

I wanted to flee, but what good would it do? I forced back my shoulders and answered. "I did, sir."

"Father, she couldn't—"

Mr. Starwyck turned a sharp glare on Lucas that stopped him mid-sentence. Then he turned back to Marlie and me, and the glare disappeared behind a smile. "And did you recognize the individuals you saw?"

I shook my head.

He rested his chin between his thumb and forefinger and seemed to think on that a moment before he spoke again. "Did you hear what they were up to? Anything about their purpose?"

"They didn't say much. Complained about the lateness of the hour, mostly. I was hiding behind a chair, so I didn't see them. But they mentioned waiting for something called a Slivering."

He squinted for a moment. "How peculiar." He bent his head down and paced the length of the shop, mulling over what I'd said. After a long moment, he looked up. "I suppose there's only one thing to do, then."

We all perked, eager to hear his plan.

A conspiratorial spark glinted in his eye as he leaned forward. "We must see if we can catch them in the act."

CHAPTER FOURTEEN

BACK IN THE kitchen, I helped Clara refashion the leftovers from the Sunday roast into a shepherd's pie. With a little mincing of the beef and a lot of mashing of the potatoes, along with some fresh carrots, peas, and gravy, the ingredients were coming together rather quickly for our traditional Monday dinner.

Too quickly, as far as I was concerned.

When the workday ended and after the kitchen cleared, Mr. Starwyck wanted Marlie and me to meet him and Lucas at Fayte Hall to try to catch the men I'd seen in the act.

It was the last thing I wanted to do, but how could I say no to the High Councilor?

Marlie wasn't any help, either. She gushed over the plan. "What an adventure!" she'd exclaimed as we returned from the wood shop.

I wished I could think of a way to call it off. What if the men I'd seen didn't show up? What if I wasted Mr. Starwyck's time? All the possible ways the night could go wrong played out in my mind as I mashed the potatoes and the minutes ticked ever closer to the dreaded moment.

I suppose it was my own fault. I never should have allowed Marlie to talk me into seeking Lucas's advice in the first place.

"If you pummel those potatoes any harder, you're going to punch a hole right through the bowl."

Clara's words startled me out of my smoldering anger, mostly because she'd been silent for more than an hour. Her light tone told me she was trying to be humorous, but even so, I could see she was on edge, too.

She'd been reading another one of her rolled-up notes when I returned from the wood shop. When she saw me, she shoved it in her pocket so quickly, it was obvious she hadn't wanted me to see it. I could only wonder why, though, because she never mentioned it.

Another hour passed with each of us locked in our own thoughts. When three large pies were finally finished and ready for the oven, she turned to me. "I need to leave a bit early this evening. Would you mind terribly if I—"

I held up my hand to stop her apology. "I don't mind cleaning up. There's not much to do, anyway." I glanced around at the dirty bowls and utensils and what was left of the herbs, butter, and cream.

The creases between her eyebrows deepened. "Are you sure it's no trouble? If it is, I could—"

"I'm absolutely sure. Is everything all right?"

She'd already untied her apron and was hanging it on the hook beside the worktable. "Yes, it's a silly little thing. A family thing. My sister."

"You don't need to explain. It's fine. Go. I'll see to things here."

"Thank you. I'll see you tomorrow, then."

As I shooed her away, I was secretly glad to have the worktable to myself. Maybe now time would slow down. I took my time delivering the pies to the oven attendants. Then gathered up the dirty bowls and utensils and took them to the washing maids myself, instead of having a kitchen page do it.

All that was left was to assemble the pantry things and return them to their places. The tiny room was empty when I entered, so instead of putting the herbs in the cupboard in the same haphazard way I'd found them, I pulled them all out and began arranging them in tidier, alphabetical rows to drag out the process.

I was making space for the star anise beside the sage when I heard voices whispering in the hall. I tried not to listen, but when I distinctly heard the name "Lucas," my ears perked. I left the herbs on the counter and moved closer to the nearly shut door, staying far enough away from the opening that I wouldn't be seen.

"It was only one night. You shouldn't let yourself get so upset over it."

It was a young woman's voice. It sounded familiar, but I couldn't place it.

"I told him at dinner I would meet him at the wood shop at nine."

I knew *that* voice without a doubt and the anger that had simmered within me for days surged to a raging boil. Ivy Coombs.

I leaned closer to listen. "If he didn't want to go for a stroll, he could have said so. He didn't say anything."

"Are you sure Lucas even heard you? Sometimes he seems... distracted." I realized that was Dinah's voice.

"Why do you always take his side?"

Ivy's whining scraped through me like chalk on a board. That simpering fool really didn't deserve someone like Lucas. Why was he even with her? With every breath, my anger ratcheted up another notch.

An idea struck...

A deliciously vengeful idea.

She might be Lucas's future bride, but I could walk out there and tell her Lucas hadn't been at the wood shop to take their moonlight stroll because he was up on at the

Purchase Cairn with me. Imagine the shock on that perfect little face of hers!

Dark satisfaction oozed through me. She deserved it, after all.

Without another thought I pulled open the door, making Ivy and Dinah whip around in surprise.

"I couldn't help but overhear your conversation," I said. Each word dripped with my rage, but then I locked eyes with Ivy and noticed how red and puffy her usually smooth porcelain skin was. I noticed two wet rivulets streaming down her cheeks.

She wiped away her tears, straightened, and tried to compose herself. "Jane, I didn't know you were there. This certainly is awkward."

"I… I…" I was going to declare why her betrothed stood her up, but my desire to hurt her—the one I'd felt up to that very moment—simply vanished. Ivy was already hurting and so terribly sad, and I didn't want to make her feel worse.

A tiny voice inside urged me on. *Do it. Tell her!*

But no, I didn't want to. And wouldn't.

"Yes? Were you going to say something?" Dinah said.

I sighed. "Yesterday was the anniversary of Lucas's mother's death. If he was out of sorts yesterday, that may have been the reason. I just thought you should know."

Ivy's expression changed from sadness to something more hopeful.

Before she could say anything more, I wished her a good night and hurried away.

~ ~ ~

The room Marlie and I shared at Balmoral was simple with no extravagances, much like the one we shared at Windsor. Two narrow beds, a chest of drawers with a washbasin, and an oval mirror hanging on the wall.

While we were here, it was home, and at the moment, it was the only place I wanted to be.

I didn't want to be around anyone.

I couldn't. I didn't trust myself after what I'd nearly done to Ivy.

I tried to make sense of it the whole way back from the kitchen. That furious rage, where had it come from? That scheme to mislead her about Lucas to cause her pain.

Something inside me wanted to do it. I thought I was that kind of person. I thought I was just like Krol, just as he said.

But when I saw the pain on her face, that thought snapped. I couldn't do it.

I didn't *want* to do it.

That's why I'd changed course and why I'd rushed out of the kitchen.

Glancing down, I realized I still had on my apron.

I untied it and draped it from one of the pegs by the door. I tugged off my gloves, went to the water pitcher, and poured some into the basin.

I submerged my hands to my wrists and kept them there, soaking in the cold. I cupped my fingers and lifted the water to my face, letting it wash over me. I repeated it again and again, as if I could wash away the darkness within me.

When I was done, when I finally felt clean and refreshed, I grabbed the small embroidered towel we kept by the bowl and wiped my eyes.

But when I opened them, the mirror was clouded over. I wiped the cloth over it to clear away the steam, but it did nothing. The blur remained. The floor swayed, and a familiar dizziness set in.

I dropped the towel, gripped the sides of the dresser, and waited for the vision.

~ ~ ~

"I just need more time, Mother." Krol stabbed his knife into a roasted mushroom and deposited it into his mouth.

The Queen remained still, except for the slight curve of her lips. "Do you think me simple, Krolaidh? You may be a prince of the Brightlands, but I will not have you sit at my table and lie to me."

He stared at her, knowing she'd seen through his charade but also knowing he could never admit such a thing. "No, Mother. I wasn't—"

Her hand shot up, and her preternaturally long fingers, terminating in silvery talon-like nails, held him frozen in an invisible grasp. At the gesture, each of the dozen guards in the room aimed the sharp end of their ten-foot spears at him and crouched, ready to attack.

How many times had he seen his mother hold traitors and political adversaries in such thrall and order her guards to end them? Too many to count. He was her only son, her baby boy, but would that matter to a queen who demanded absolute allegiance? Demanded it from all, that is, except his sister. How Druansha managed to evade their mother's wrath he had yet to discover.

"What is the point, anyway?" his mother spat. "You will outlive the girl by centuries. She will wither and die before you even reach your prime, so why bother?"

How could he make her see she was wrong? She would never understand. She couldn't. Whatever understanding she might have had died with his father so long ago no one even remembered the old king's name. So, he wouldn't fight his mother. It would be easier to pretend than to prolong the pain.

And there was always pain, she made sure of that. Even now, she strangled the breath from him, making him choke and gasp. She savored his humiliation, no doubt.

Once she was satisfied by his torture, she lowered her hand and released the hold. He nearly collapsed into his plate before recovering himself.

"Thank you, Mother," he grumbled aloud, knowing she was waiting for his show of gratitude, however false it might be. Sincerity *was never important to her, after all. Sometimes he wondered if she'd even recognize it anymore.*

"*Of course, my darling. Now what would you like to say?*"

He locked on her unwavering gaze. "*It will be done. I swear to you.*"

She sat back into the embrace of her chair. "*Very good. Let that be the end of it, then.*"

CHAPTER FIFTEEN

LUCAS BENT HIS ear to the Fayte Hall door and listened. I leaned in beside him.

"I don't hear anything," I said. "Do you?"

He shook his head.

"Can we please hurry?" Marlie peered over her shoulder at the darkness behind us. "We can't let them see us."

"There's no reason to worry, Miss Carlisle," Mr. Starwyck said while maintaining a polite distance, so he wouldn't inadvertently brush by me. "We have every right to be here."

His words gave me confidence, and I felt better knowing we had the High Councilor with us.

I couldn't say the same for Lucas. He hardly acknowledged his father as we made our way down. Now, he focused every ounce of his attention on the door as he positioned his Faytling in the lock. In a heartbeat, the familiar click and grind of the mechanisms within the wall released. After a quick glance around, he motioned for us to follow and pulled the door closed behind him.

The darkness engulfed us, except for the dim glow of

the little candle I held, which struggled even more here than it had guiding us through the tunnel. It had been a challenge to make our way along the route that way, but triggering the tunnel's lights would have risked having our presence discovered by the footman we were trying catch. Lighting the gas lamps and hearth would do the same, so we remained huddled around the solitary flame with the humming, rumbling sound of the air apparatus hard at work.

The creak of a door set my nerves on edge. I spun around, fearing we'd already been caught. But it wasn't the door. Marlie had opened the wardrobe and was pulling out garments.

"What are you doing?" I gaped in disbelief. The formality seemed a waste of time under the circumstances.

Lucas grabbed one from her and pulled it on. "It's probably a good idea. We might need to blend in."

"Capital idea," Mr. Starwyck said, accepting a robe for himself.

I grudgingly took one. "Fine. But if we need to blend in, it means we have bigger problems."

Lucas ignored my comment and tossed his hood back. "Show me where you found the hidden doorway."

I fastened my robe and pointed in the direction of the paneled wall across from the staircase. "Over there."

"That's impossible." He sneered but moved toward the wall anyway and ran his fingertips along the molding.

"I'll show you." I set down the candle and pressed the center of the space with my palm. With a soft click, the camouflaged doorway sprang away from the wall.

"That shouldn't be there," Lucas said. He looked to his father. "Did you know this was here?"

Mr. Starwyck looked as surprised as his son.

Lucas examined the door jamb. "This should be a reinforced wall."

"Remember, someone is down there," I whispered.

He nodded and followed Marlie, Mr. Starwyck, and me down the staircase. I led the way with the candle.

At the bottom, we could see a corridor to the right, and the stairwell's wood paneling gave way to earthen walls and a dirt floor.

"Is that a light down there?" Marlie asked.

It was faint but definitely a light. I raised my finger to my lips, extinguished the candle, and padded softly to have a look. Along the way, we passed openings to what might be alcoves or chambers on both sides of the corridor. But the light was coming from the far end, and unless my eyes were playing tricks on me, it was getting brighter.

When we reached it, we found a room set off at a sharp angle, which allowed only a fraction of the light to flow back our direction.

I craned my head around and saw Boudica's chalice at the center of the chamber with a ring of candles standing in water-filled bowls around it. A robed figure, a man by the size of him, walked the ring, murmuring words I didn't understand and lighting each candle with the flame of a long and slender torch.

I pulled back before he could see me and motioned for the others to retreat. As we headed back the way we'd come, we heard voices coming from the staircase.

Marlie pulled me closer. "What do we do now?"

"Follow me." Lucas pulled us into the dark opening of a smaller chamber. We felt our way through the shadows and discovered several crates pushed into a corner. We huddled behind them in the darkness. Since the candle was no help, I dropped it and lifted my Faytling, silently urging it to glow.

"How did you do that?" Marlie hissed in my ear when a pinkish light pulsed within it.

Mr. Starwyck edged closer, as though he wanted to know as well.

I'd forgotten lighting a Faytling wasn't a common skill

among the Guardians, and I wished I hadn't done it. "It just happened one day, by accident."

Mr. Starwyck frowned and rubbed his jaw. He didn't believe me, I could tell.

Marlie tugged her Faytling from beneath her blouse and lifted it, as though trying to light hers as well. "Ask it to light, using your thoughts," I whispered.

It did as the voices neared. I wrapped my fingers around my Faytling to mute its light, and Marlie did the same.

"No trouble at all," a man said to another as he passed the entrance to our hiding place. "No one suspects anything as far as I can tell."

"Good, that should give us time."

Was it the same men I'd overheard before? I wasn't sure because I was too focused on the thumping of my heart. I knew I shouldn't be afraid—we had Mr. Starwyck with us, after all—but I couldn't shake the feeling we were in danger.

We watched a procession of robed figures pass by us. I counted ten, but the shadows cast by their candles made it nearly impossible to distinguish one silhouette from another.

Still, it was enough to rattle my nerves. Marlie's expression told me she felt the same. Even with the High Councilor's help, they could overpower us, if given the opportunity.

I hoped beyond hope they wouldn't get that opportunity.

"I think that's all of them," Lucas whispered when the corridor cleared. "We need to go back to see what they're doing."

He was right, but every part of me was begging to leave this place, screaming that it wasn't safe. I loosened my grip on my Faytling, letting some of its light free.

"My son has a point. We need to see for ourselves, or

we haven't accomplished anything."

Neither Starwyck waited for Marlie or me to agree. They rustled their way from behind the crates and made their way toward the corridor.

"The coast is clear," Lucas whispered after peering out. "I don't see anyone else coming."

I watched their shadows disappear into the corridor.

"They're right," I whispered to Marlie, who like me hadn't moved. "We won't know what they're doing if we don't have a look."

"Fine," she said. "But we better not get caught. I really don't want to get caught."

Neither did I. "Even if they do, they won't do anything to us. We have Mr. Starwyck on our side."

The closer we got, the more clearly we could hear the discussion in progress.

"The Fayte Guardians have lost their way," a man bellowed. It was the one who had shouted at me before, but I knew that nasally arrogance. I knew that voice!

"Our leaders," he continued, "have been blinded; they've lost their way. They no longer abide by the Fayte Covenant. They don't even remember it. Do you?"

There was a low murmuring of assent.

"That Covenant," the orator declared, "lies not in serving a throne, but in guarding this land."

Those last three words rang out with reverence and set off another round of murmurs.

"Do not forget," he continued, "our ancestors were given the sacred gifts to protect the countryside from invaders. We pledged our gifts to mortal sovereigns, but to what end? Our Queen now reaches beyond the British Isles. She turns her attention to the other side of the world and away from her purpose. *Our* true purpose, Guardians."

My heart stopped.

Marlie was close enough I could hear her breath. "Do you think he's talking about India?"

I nodded.

Someone shouted, "Yeah," and the grumblings and agitation grew stronger.

"Yes," the orator said. "It's unfortunate but true. What this Queen calls an Empire, I call an abomination. It's an abdication of her Divine Right. She no longer puts our country first. Guardians, she has broken the Fayte Covenant, and the Lady does nothing. The Lady has grown weak; that's why *we* have grown weak."

A new round of discontented grunts echoed through the corridor.

"I say, Guardians, it is time we pledge a new allegiance to one who will return our strength to us and our true purpose."

The supportive mumblings broke into outright cheers.

"Are you ready to make that pledge with me, Guardians?"

More cheers.

"Close the circle around the flames to witness the power of our new liege."

There was shuffling, and I imagined them moving around Boudica's vessel and the candles. I didn't have to see to know what was coming next. Krol was close. I could feel him like heat rolling off a fire and filling these rooms.

Marlie turned back again, her eyes wide with panic.

I motioned to Mr. Starwyck. He was the High Councilor; we couldn't move until he permitted it, though honestly I don't know why he hadn't already stopped this travesty.

Lucas caught my eye. I could see he shared my concern.

"Shouldn't we do something?" I whispered.

He leaned into his father's ear, but the man flicked him away.

Lucas looked back at me with a sheepish shrug. I probably should have held my place, and maybe I would have if it weren't for Clara's words: *Don't always do what you're told.*

That advice had resonated with me in the kitchen, and it rang through me now. Mr. Starwyck may be the High Councilor, but he'd never faced Krol. He didn't know the dark power these rogue Guardians were inviting into this world.

But I did.

Quickly, before Lucas or Marlie could stop me, I pushed to the front of our group and planted myself in the doorway. "Stop! You're making a terrible mistake."

The man who'd been leading the ceremony regarded me, as did every other robed figure in the room, of which I quickly tallied twelve. I searched the blackness beneath the leader's hood for his identity, but his face was hidden in shadow. I searched the other faces, but they kept their faces hidden as well.

"You should not be here," the leader said, his voice echoing off the earthen walls.

"Me?" I bellowed back. "I know who you are Edward Bailey."

He straightened and seemed surprised to be called out. He lifted a hand to his hood and pushed it back. For a moment, I feared I'd gotten it wrong.

But no, I recognized that sharp chin and the bushy gray mustache upon his lip. That was the menace who had fled from Windsor Castle. There was no mistaking it.

My panic subsided by degrees. "You won't get away this time. The High Councilor is here. He's seen everything."

Yes, I was gloating. He'd thought himself so clever, but we'd trapped him. I waited for Mr. Starwyck to step forward to tell them himself.

Mr. Bailey's lips slid into a mocking grin. "Do you really believe that?"

As he said it, the water in Boudica's chalice bubbled. A

reddish mist rose from the surface and flowed over the sides to the floor.

The air crackled with the anticipation of the surrounding Guardians.

How stupid they were. They had no idea what was happening, but I did, and I wouldn't allow it. I whipped around to my friends. "We have to leave. He's coming. It isn't safe here."

Even now I could feel Krol's power gathering. Before today I might have welcomed it. I might even have believed as these fools did that he offered something better. But not now. Rage and hate and greed, that's all he was. He'd nearly made me that, too, but not now. I would not choose that path.

I wanted to run, but I couldn't leave the others. They had no idea what they were about to face.

"We have to get out of here!" I pushed at Marlie's and Lucas's backs, but they wouldn't budge. Mr. Starwyck stood in their way, and he wouldn't move.

"Sir," I called. "We can't fight him. I don't even know how to stop him. We must leave before it's too late!"

Why wasn't he moving? Had fear paralyzed the man?

Then I saw it: that glint in his eye. It wasn't panic, it was amusement. He called out, "May I have some assistance over here?"

Three of the closest Guardians broke from their ranks and grabbed us, pulling us back toward the wide metal goblet, still billowing steam like the diving pool.

"Mr. Starwyck," Mr. Bailey said, "I see you've brought our guests."

"Of course, Mr. Bailey. I hope we haven't kept you waiting long."

"Your timing couldn't be better," Mr. Bailey said.

"What's happening here?" It was the question I was thinking, but the words belonged to Lucas. He was staring at his father with a mixture of fear and disgust. "What have you done?"

"Be quiet, boy." Mr. Starwyck sneered at him. I could hardly believe this was the same man who'd helped us. He was one of them?

Had I been that blind? A flood of memories came back, especially the way he always remained out of reach. A touch could give him away, that's why he'd been so careful. He'd been part of this scheme from the start.

All at once, the robed figures that surrounded us lowered to one knee, even Mr. Bailey and Mr. Starwyck. Only Marlie, Lucas, and I stood. My friends gaped at the column forming in the crimson mist, for in the center of it a human form was taking shape, one I knew all too well. Krol emerged, his bare granite shoulders and his black hair hanging loose down his back. When he swept around, his fiery serpent gaze found me.

My daughter.

Had he said the words aloud, or had they only been in my head? I searched the faces of my friends, but they registered only fear. For that I was glad, but I was sure my secret wasn't safe.

"Is that... Is that the creature?" Marlie's words tripped over her panic. The rogue Guardian loosened his grip, but she didn't move. Lucas didn't, either. They were in shock, and I didn't blame them.

Someone laughed, but it wasn't Krol. Mr. Starwyck stood, with his hands clasped behind his back. It wasn't happy laughter, but something far more sinister. "I must applaud you, Miss Shackle. You've done us a great service."

"I've done nothing for you," I spat.

He strolled the room's perimeter. "But you have, my dear. You have saved us the trouble of ridding ourselves of you."

At that, Mr. Bailey laughed, and I saw he'd risen from his knees as well, as had the others. "I wanted to stop you the first time you stuck your nose through that door, but Mr. Starwyck knew better. He knew you'd find your way here. It's in your nature, he said. By the time the Queen arrives, everything will be ready."

"You knew we'd come?" Of course, he did. It had been Mr. Starwyck's plan. I spun around and glared at him. "You did this?"

"I made the suggestion, that's true," he said. "But you would have managed it on your own eventually. How could you resist? You would be drawn to your own father, wouldn't you? You know, I think I can see the family resemblance."

"Leave Jane alone!" Marlie's outcry made him laugh again.

She kicked at the rogue Guardian who was holding her from behind. She tried to shrug her way out of the man's grasp, but he was too strong. "You're evil," she insisted. "You've betrayed the Fayte. You've betrayed the Lady."

Krol had been standing silent, watching this, but at the mention of Druansha, he sneered. The crimson mist deepened to an even darker shade.

"Watch what you say, girl," Mr. Bailey warned. "Our liege has a hunger for souls, and we could easily part with yours."

I listened for Krol's response but saw only the flame ignited in his eyes.

"Don't threaten her," Lucas said and tried to yank his arms free from his captor. He didn't succeed.

"My, my, how brave you are young Starwyck," Mr. Bailey mocked. "I assure you that you have nothing to fear. There's so little left of your soul, it would hardly be worth the effort."

"My soul is just fine, thank you," Lucas spat at him.

"Mr. Bailey." Mr. Starwyck turned his glare on the man. His meaning was clear: stop talking.

But Mr. Bailey wasn't the one Mr. Starwyck needed to

worry about. The way Krol was watching the man, I could see something brewing within him. The mist billowed and swirled around him, and then he stepped out of it, as solid as any of us and looking more the warrior than he ever had.

The Guardians gasped and stepped back. Fresh fear etched deep on their faces.

"My liege, you walk among us." Mr. Bailey's eyes betrayed his astonishment. Had he not planned on such a thing? I wondered what he had expected.

"My patience is nearing its end." Krol reached his powerful arms to his sides, stretching and flexing the muscles as if he'd just awakened. Then he held one arm out toward Mr. Bailey, and from his fingers, a flash of red fire shot like a twisted rope and wrapped itself around Mr. Bailey's neck. It wound again and again, cutting off his breath.

The man squirmed and fought to free himself, but the tether tightened like a noose. A choking, gurgling sound emerged from him and his eyes bulged. After what seemed like an eternity, he went limp. His frantic eyes dulled as his life drained away.

We all stared in horror.

Do you see how they cower? How weak they are?

It was his voice in my head. I wanted to cover my ears, to scream at him to leave me alone, but I couldn't without giving myself away.

Krol hardly seemed concerned with me, however. As he strode through the circle like a medieval gargoyle sprung to life, he watched Mr. Starwyck. When he stopped in front of the man, he said, "You've done well. Your sacrifice has been duly rewarded, has it not?"

Mr. Starwyck's eyes darted to Lucas, who was watching with growing alarm. "What sacrifice, Father? What did you do?"

Krol regarded Lucas then turned back to his father.

"The boy doesn't know?"

Lucas was hardly a boy, but the term seemed intended to diminish him.

"Know what, Father? What should I know?" His voice cracked with a fear that bordered on hysteria.

"It wasn't necessary," Mr. Starwyck replied coolly.

"Of course." A hint of a smile played on Krol's blackened lips. "But tell me, does he suspect? Surely he must."

Mr. Starwyck's stoic expression weakened. His jaw tensed, but he said nothing.

Lucas appeared too stunned to speak.

Krol, however, was taking it all in. The more discomfort he caused, the more he seemed to enjoy himself. "I must confess," he said, "I thought it would kill him. I'm pleased to see that wasn't the case."

"You wanted to kill me?" Even in the candlelight, I could see Lucas go white. Perhaps I had, too.

Krol approached him. "No, boy, he didn't want to kill you." Though his voice was consoling, I knew it was a trick. I saw the fire in his reptilian eyes. "He merely did as I required in return for a favor." He turned to Mr. Starwyck. "Isn't that so, *High Councilor*?"

Lucas stopped struggling against his constraints and stared up at the creature. He swallowed hard. "What did you require?"

Every eye in the room locked onto these two. Every breath stopped, eager for the answer.

Krol glanced around. He knew this was his moment, and he drew it out. When he was ready, he held out his hands and said, "I simply required a Sliver of your soul."

CHAPTER SIXTEEN

"YOU TOOK MY soul?" Lucas struggled with the words. He swung around to face his father. "You did that to me? How could you?"

Mr. Starwyck didn't answer. He wouldn't even look at his son. Instead, he stared at the chalice still shrouded in mist at the center of the room.

Lucas wasn't giving up. "Why did you even send me to Windsor? Did you know it was a fool's errand?"

"It served its purpose," his father sneered.

Krol had been holding back, watching the exchange with interest, but now he stepped forward. "Tell me, young Starwyck, did you not notice the absence? Did you feel no difference?"

The Slivering made sense now. It was the morsel Krol had been ordered to take from my mother in my vision. He'd already taken it from Lucas, and now he intended to take it from the Queen. I winced at the horror of it.

Lucas was having a different reaction. His strength was returning to him and his rage along with it. "What have you done with my soul? I want it back."

Krol stalked the cavernous room. "I assure you, it is

only a small portion, and it is quite safe in the Brightlands."

That strangely luminescent place he'd shown me? How did it get there?

"I want it back!" Lucas's lips trembled, but not from tears. Something far more violent was working through him. "I want what you stole from me." Somehow, he wrenched himself free from his captor's grasp, and he ran at Krol, colliding into him with such force it sent both careening to the center of the room. Krol collapsed against the metal goblet, splashing its contents onto the candles around it, extinguishing most of them and dimming the room to near darkness.

In the cluster of robes and rushing feet, it was impossible to see who was where, but from somewhere in that cacophony, I heard a distinct roar then Mr. Starwyck wailed, "The mist is disappearing. Hurry, we need water for our liege!"

Several Guardians rushed to the spilled mess, some dropped to their knees and dragged their cupped hands through the muddy puddles, trying to retrieve what they could.

I searched for Krol and thought I found his red serpent eyes in the darkness, but it was only a scarlet wisp of smoke that seemed to cling to a tree root that was... no, that couldn't be. I blinked and stared again, and still it seemed the root was slithering along the wall like a giant snake above all this chaos.

Lucas yelled, "Run!"

Whether he saw what I saw or something else, I didn't wait to ask. I yanked free of the Guardian holding me, and as everyone else scrambled, I made my way through the melee and hoped Lucas and Marlie were already ahead of me.

"Find them!" an angry voice called out. It had to be Mr. Starwyck, but it was impossible to know for sure.

"Don't let them get away!"

I heard feet running, searching. The corridor was nearly pitch black, and I hoped it would hide me until I could make it to the staircase.

Behind, I heard footsteps closing in. I'd never make it to the stairs. So instead, I felt along the wall for the first opening and slipped inside. Using my hands as guides, I searched in front of me for crates or something to give me cover. My plan was to sneak out after my pursuers passed by.

I wasn't so lucky. A robed figure holding one of the candles from the room stopped at the door, just inches from the crates that hid me.

"I know you're in here," a raspy voice whispered. "You aren't getting away."

Maybe not, but I wouldn't go willingly, either. I pressed both hands against the top crate and pushed with every ounce of strength left to me. Whatever that crate held wasn't heavy, so it went flying at the man's face and knocked him backward. He dropped the candle and grabbed his head before slumping to the floor. I don't know if he was unconscious or not, but I ran past him as fast as I could. I ran, blinded again by the darkness, to the staircase and ascended the steps two and three at a time.

At the door, I paused, chest heaving with gasping breaths. I leaned close to listen before throwing it open.

Voices. Low murmurs I couldn't make out, but there were definitely people on the other side. Defeated, I slumped to the ground.

How could I come this far only to fail?

No, I rejected the thought. I couldn't give up. I still had a chance.

But what could I do? Hide in an alcove? Wait until the coast was clear? It wasn't a great plan, but it was all I had.

Before I retreated, I unlatched the door and held it. When I was sure it wouldn't swing open, I raced back down the staircase.

There were more voices in the still black corridor. They'd found my pursuer and were cursing my name.

"We've got the boy and one of the girls," someone cried out.

"Don't let any of them get away!" It was Mr. Starwyck.

How could he be so cruel? I thought back to what Lucas had said about the man hating him, and I regretted having my doubts. His father was as much a monster as Krol.

I felt along the walls and slid into the first room I came to. I made my way back, running my palms along the hard-packed earth until I came to a cabinet pushed against the wall. I nudged it forward so I could hide behind it, but what I found there wasn't a wall but a small opening.

An even better place to hide!

I pushed the cabinet farther until enough of the opening was exposed that I could wriggle through. When I did, I tried to find the back wall, but it was deeper than I'd thought. When I heard a group of Guardians rushing through the corridor, they sounded so far away, and I couldn't see them at all.

How large was this room?

I kept moving along the curve. When I couldn't hear the voices anymore, I pulled my Faytling from beneath my collar and asked for its light. Its pinkish glow revealed no end to the wall in front of me. Another tunnel?

I glanced back toward the corridor. I could go back, but I was certain to be discovered if I did.

It left only one choice. With the Faytling to light my way, I was better off venturing into the unknown.

~ ~ ~

I hurried through the tunnel, not caring where it led. At first, I knew I was traveling north, but after several curves,

I lost all sense of direction. I clutched my side, where a stitch was making my stride unsteady. Then a tree root that jutted up through the soil caught my toe and sent me crashing to the ground.

Pain exploded in my right ankle. It was all I could do not to cry out. Instead, I shoved my fist against my lips and swallowed the agony because I didn't know where I was or who might hear me.

When I tried to rise, the pain knocked me back down. I pulled up my knees and rested my forehead against them. Sitting there, I mulled my options. Part of me wanted to give up, just sink down against the cold earth and accept defeat.

But what would happen to Marlie and Lucas? No one in the castle knew where they were. No one even knew they were in danger.

I had to get free of this tunnel and find help, at least for their sake.

Grabbing at a tangle of tree roots, I hoisted myself up from the ground, taking care to keep as much weight on my left foot as possible. The pain nearly doubled me over again, but I managed to stay upright and then, in halting steps, to move.

But the unfortunate truth was, I didn't know where this tunnel led, or if it led anywhere at all. What if I was headed for a dead end?

That question hounded me as I limped on, fighting back the hurt and my doubts. As the cold, fresh air gave way to the smell of wet soil and decaying roots and leaves, my doubts multiplied. The rancid scent of rotting things permeated the stagnant air, and every breath brought me closer to the conviction that I'd made a terrible mistake.

I was about to turn back when the ground gently slopped upward and gave me hope.

How long had I been moving? An hour, four hours? I'd lost all sense of time, but it didn't matter. I was near the end, I had to be.

I raised my Faytling, and its dim light glanced off two giant rocks jutting up against each other, blocking what had to be the exit.

I'd come this far to find this?

Disappointment, frustration, and anger surged through me, but I didn't have the strength to turn back, at least not yet. I needed to rest, but the ground that had been dusty and dry was now muddy. I could see water trickling between the rocks, probably from a recent rain.

Then I smelled it: the sweet scent of fresh, forest air. I gulped it in, filling my lungs. I stumbled closer to the rocks. Even if I couldn't get out, I could at least breathe this glorious air.

As I neared, I saw the rocks weren't wedged against each other as they'd appeared. They weren't even rocks at all. Instead, they were the gnarled contours of a massive yew tree, and as I grew closer, my Faytling brightened, and what had appeared to be a seam between boulders was now widening and becoming a dark, yawning space. It wasn't large, but large enough for me to squeeze through.

I poked my head out to see what was on the other side and found a dense but dark grove. The thick canopy of leaves and branches hid the moon and obscured the night sky, but I didn't care. I was out!

Somewhere in the distance, a bird squawked a complaint at the sound of my movement, and a light twinkled over the rise of low hills. Was it a window at Balmoral Castle? It was too far and too dark to know for sure, but it didn't matter. I was out of that tunnel, and I was free from Krol and the Guardians.

But even if I was safe, Marlie and Lucas weren't. That meant I had to keep moving.

My gut told me to go north. I turned that way and limped as best I could. One step, then another. Each more painful than the last.

I don't know how long I went on that way. Another hour, two? But I couldn't stop. I'd never find help for Marlie and Lucas if I did. That thought carried me on. With every step I thought of them, but as time slipped by, and what was left of my strength with it, the reality of my situation set in: I was lost in these woods. I had no idea where I was going, and there was little, if any chance I'd ever make it out, not alive, anyway.

My toe caught on another tree root and sent me tumbling to the ground, face first. This time, I didn't try to get up. I stretched out upon the muddy path, closed my eyes, and let consciousness slip away.

CHAPTER SEVENTEEN

KROL SETTLED BACK against the tree and watched Madeleine toss pebbles along the stream, trying to land one beyond a branch that had fallen across the ravine nearly a dozen yards away. It was a game she had played most of the afternoon as they sat beside the rushing water. Or, rather, she had played because he was still trying to decide how to say what he'd come to say.

"There, did you see that? I made it over." Her smile brightened her whole face, even in the moonlight. He never tired of it, and they'd been meeting for nearly a fortnight, usually at dusk when she should have been taking her meal break. Or, if she couldn't get away then, she'd come later, sometimes in the dead of night when she should have been fast asleep.

Krol nodded then went back to staring at the hills in the distance.

She nudged his arm, pulling his attention back to her.

"What causes that frown, my sweet?" She touched his cheek.

He pulled away and glanced off. The time had come, whether he was ready for it or not. "I need to ask you something," he said.

She dropped the pebble she was about to throw. "What is it?"

He stared at a patch of grass below the rocks on which they sat. He'd been trying to come up with the right words, but it was no use. He couldn't tell her the truth, so he'd decided to be vague to make it

138

easier on her. "It's about my mother."

She toyed with the pebbles. "You've never spoken of her. What's she like?"

The muscles around his jaw tightened. He sat upright, leaving the languid position beside her. Why was he dragging this out? He should have already said what he came to say and been done with it. He just couldn't bring himself to do it. "She is… difficult," he said at last.

An amused sigh rose from her petal pink lips. "Aren't all mothers?"

"Yes, of course." He swallowed, making his Adam's apple bob sharply. "She's discovered that I've been meeting you here. She wants… to meet you."

Laughter bubbled from her. "Is that so terrible?" Something close to pride lightened her voice, but Krol's only darkened.

He closed his eyes and turned away. "I'm afraid it will be."

Again, Madeleine only laughed and sent another pebble skimming across the stream.

~ ~ ~

A stick poked my shoulder and pulled me from oblivion. A soft tap and then another.

"Wake up, my dear. This isn't the time for sleeping."

Was it Madeleine? No, that had been a dream, and it was already fading. This was a gentle voice, an older voice, but not one I knew.

Another tap, more insistent this time.

"Come now. Wake up."

My eyes cracked open, and I could see someone hovering above. The moonlight behind her kept her in silhouette, but the soft voice comforted me. It promised warmth and safety, and perhaps another descent into nothingness.

"No, no. You must get up." The gentle prodding pressed more urgently. "They'll be searching for you."

They?

The crimson mist. Krol in that traitorous ceremony before disappearing as a wisp of red smoke. Mr. Starwyck's betrayal. All of it came rushing back.

The woman's stick dug into my back.

"That hurts!" The pain brought awareness. I could see her better now. Head shrouded by a wool shawl that draped over her shoulders. A rough cloak brushed against me, dark as the night and smelling of fresh bread and roasted meats.

My stomach growled. When had I last eaten?

The woman bent closer to peer at me, and that savory fragrance drifted to my nose from her fingers. "Get up," she whispered again harshly. "They're coming now. I can see the torches. We must go."

I knew who was coming. Mr. Starwyck. The rogue Guardians. Maybe Krol himself.

I thought of Marlie and Lucas caught in choke holds. They hadn't gotten away. I knew that, though I didn't know how. My chin dropped to my chest, and I nearly wept.

"No time for that now, dove. We have to go!"

The old woman was pushing me with her stick, urging me to my feet, but she didn't have the strength. Finally, I accepted what she already knew. We were both in danger.

If it were only me, I might have surrendered. Let them drag me back and leave me to whatever fate awaited my friends. But I couldn't subject this woman to that. She was trying to help, even if I refused.

"Leave me alone." I tried to shoo her away, to send her off to safety.

"Not without you, Jane. There is no hope without you."

How did she know my name? I looked at her and tried to see into the dark space of the shawl obscuring her face. "Do I know you?"

She shook her head. "But I know you. I'm Lavinia Bellington."

The name resonated. This was my mother's sister. Clara and Ada's mother. But what was she doing in the middle of the forest? "How did you find me?"

"The trees told me you were coming."

"The trees?"

"Yes. They have much to say if you know how to listen, and they've had much to say about you. They say you need help, and if you don't get up and start moving, you're going to need a lot more than that." She craned her head up to check our surroundings.

I didn't know if I could believe her, but what choice did I have?

The sound of yelling in the distance worried me as well.

"They're going the other way for now," she said, "but we must go."

Her instructions were still sifting through my muddled thoughts. Could I trust this woman? Was she yet another traitor among the Fayte Guardians? It was a terrible thing to think of Clara and Ada's mother, but after Mr. Starwyck's deception, I didn't trust my instincts. I had to be cautious. "If the trees told you, won't they tell them, as well?"

She scoffed. "The trees could yell at those muttonheads all day long, and they'd never hear a thing. They've lost their magic. They've lost all their good sense, too, if you ask me. Now get up and let's go. Before it's too late."

I pulled myself up by the side of a rock but when I put weight on my right foot, I nearly doubled over in pain.

Mrs. Bellington gazed down at it.

"Oh, my. That is a problem."

Above the rim of my boot, my limb had swollen nearly twice its normal size. It was monstrous.

"Here, take the stick." She reached out, offering me the staff she'd used to prod me. The extra leverage kept me steady but did nothing for the pain.

"This way. Keep your head low, if you can. We've got a ways to go."

We pushed through the densest part of the forest for what seemed like hours, but in truth I'd lost all sense of time.

All the while, the old woman muttered to herself, speaking to the trees or to ghosts, I couldn't tell which.

"Maybe the Lady could help us?" I had no right to ask for Druansha's help, and I didn't know if she would offer any, but I was desperate.

"The Lady? And how do you suppose we ask her?" There was a mocking tone in her voice.

"You just do. I've done it before."

Mrs. Bellington glowered at me. "In the Sanctum, you mean?"

I regretted saying anything. "Yes, of course, that's what I meant." My voice faded to a whisper. I didn't want to reveal more than I should. All I knew about this woman was what Clara had told me, and that wasn't much.

"We have no Sanctum here, and I've warded this place to keep us unseen from the Brightlanders. If we tried calling her, it would break the ward. It's too risky."

"The Brightlanders?"

"Yes, yes. The others like the Lady. They aren't to be trusted, you know. Capricious and wicked, they are."

I nodded. That certainly did describe Krol. She feared him, that was a good sign. But if she knew more about me, perhaps she'd fear me, too. I kept the thought to myself.

"Hurry." She ducked into a thicket and disappeared behind the leaves.

I hesitated.

A hand reached out. It was her hand, and she grabbed my sleeve. "Come now," she said from the other side.

I followed, leaning on the staff as much as I could, and discovered after an unpleasant encounter with the sharp ends of several twigs and branches that the ground sloped downward and we were walking through a dry ravine hidden by the brush.

A good while later, Mrs. Bellington stopped and touched an exposed root. Her eyes closed and fluttered. She took a long, deep breath, and the worry melted from her expression. "It's safe now. They've gone another way."

I stared at her hand. "That tree root told you that?"

Her head bobbled as though she wasn't sure how she wanted to answer then nodded, weakly. "More like it showed me. But no matter, we can take the rest at a more relaxed pace."

"How much farther are we going?"

"Not far. This way."

When we came to a clearing, I saw a small hovel of a house. A tiny thing nearly hidden between two yew trees with low, bushy branches. In the moonlight, I could see two small windows adorned the front and pansies grew beside the door.

Once we were inside and she'd lighted a candle, she led me to a cot in the back and lay me down on a pillow before lifting my good foot and unlacing my boot. I tensed at her touch and braced for a vision.

She patted my leg. "No need for that. You're safe here."

Instead of a vision, a shuddering light appeared to me, a tiny speck that grew bit by bit until it was all I could see.

I could no longer see Mrs. Bellington or her home. I couldn't see anything. My only awareness was the feeling of drifting toward that light until it was all around me. Within it, one moment flowed into another, one sensation into another, until all of it blended into an endless circle of white.

CHAPTER EIGHTEEN

THE MOON RESTED low on the horizon and hid its face behind a ridge of trees when Krol found Madeleine beside the stream. He paused in the shadows and observed her. She'd brought her carpetbag, just as he'd asked. Good. When her disappearance was noticed, her people would assume she'd run off. No one would suspect the truth.

Everything was going according to Mother's plan.

Then Madeleine pulled the pins from her hair and let the long, dark waves fall around her shoulders. The way her hair glistened in the scant moonlight made him ache to run his fingers through those strands once more. To hold her once more. The desire consumed him.

When she turned and saw him watching from the oak, her smile shined brighter than any star. Her happiness eclipsed every other thought and hooked him somewhere deep inside.

That's when he knew.

He wouldn't do Mother's bidding. He wasn't going to take Madeleine's soul to the Brightlands. He wouldn't do anything to harm her or remove even a whisper of her phantom spirit.

But when he returned empty-handed, there would be consequences. He'd be banished from court and left to rot in the Gray Woods. Exile from the Brightlands and the Queen's protection was a fate he couldn't even imagine.

Without Mother's light, without her grace, he would lose himself, eventually. They always did.

But his choice was made. He couldn't go back. Not ever. He only had to make Madeleine understand. They would find a way to be together in this world. Somehow.

Trepidation filled him. Could he really do it? Could he ignore Mother as his sister did?

His resolve weakened.

Madeleine looked up at him then, and there was such sweetness in her heavenly blue eyes. The human capacity to love and be loved still surprised him. He could never leave this woman behind. She was his life now and the only thing that truly mattered.

~ ~ ~

A pigeon cooed nearby and startled me awake, making the unsettling images of Krol and my mother fade from my mind. I didn't remember drifting off, but I must have been asleep for some time because bright sunlight streamed through the open windows.

The coo came again, and I spied her, a small blue-gray pigeon on the windowsill beyond the foot of my bed. Her head jerked, then she gazed upon me with her tawny eyes and cooed again.

"Hello there." I had intended to say the words, but what came out was a strangely garbled sound. The edges of my lips twitched into what I wanted to be a smile, but I wasn't sure I'd accomplished that, either.

The pigeon didn't seem to mind. She hopped along the sill then flew away.

I squinted at what I could see of the sky. Was it morning or afternoon?

Something rustled beside me.

"So, you're awake. Yes, that's good. I was beginning to wonder."

I turned to see the back of a roundish woman with a

silver braid that nearly touched the bottom tie of her apron. I recognized the voice. She'd found me in the forest and brought me here.

"Yes, I brought you here. You're safe. They won't find you. I've made sure of it."

I hadn't spoken aloud. How could she possibly...

"I have my ways."

This one-sided conversation reminded me of my own with...

I mentally dropped the thought.

"It's all right. I already know."

A deep dread came over me. I closed my eyes and retreated into the dark space again.

"There's no need for that. We've all got our secrets, haven't we?"

Her voice was still chipper. It eased my guilt.

The woman leaned over and tucked the blanket around me. "The way I see it, he only had a hand in your beginning. How you end up and where your future takes you, that's entirely up to you. It's what you do now that matters."

Her words were a comfort, but they also fired my curiosity. If she knew about my father, she must also know my mother. I held the thought in my mind, waiting for her to read it.

"You have had a difficult time of it, haven't you?" she said. "Harder than most, to be sure."

Was she talking about my mother? My thinking was still muddled, but I tried to focus on the thought, waiting for her to say more.

Instead, she tapped my knee lightly over the bedcovers. "You'll be up and around again in no time." Then she rose and busied herself by clearing away what looked like her morning dishes from the table, leaving me with my frustrated hopes.

When she finished, she returned with her hands

wrapped in dish towels and helped me lean forward to make room for additional pillows behind me, so I could properly sit up. Her caution should have put me at ease, but it did the opposite. Was she being careful not to touch me out of concern for me or herself?

"There, that's better. Clear the head. How's that feel?"

"All right." It was easier to speak now, and I could see more clearly. Since I couldn't coax her into speaking about my mother and she didn't seem inclined to share anything on that subject, I took stock of the cottage, taking in the simple room with the bed at one end and a hearth at the other. There was a ladder near the middle that ascended to a loft where I could see the corner of another bed. That must be where she slept.

The place was tidy. The curtains and furnishings were old but well tended. A fire in the hearth warmed the bottom of a black kettle.

"Where am I?" My voice cracked.

"There's nothing for you to worry about. You're safe. They can't find you. No one can find you."

I thought of Krol.

"Not even him." She gave me a long, knowing look that brought a hot flush over my cheeks.

"How do you know about him?" I tried to make the question strong, but it came out in a whisper.

"Let's talk about that later, shall we? You've been through so much, and you have much healing yet to do. How's that foot feeling, by the way?"

I tried to move my foot. It hurt, but not nearly as much as I remembered. I lifted the white muslin corset cover I was wearing, a garment I didn't recognize but which fit me nonetheless. My foot and ankle were still swollen and had become a kaleidoscope of grays and blues, greens and yellows. "How long have I been here?"

"Six days. No, sorry, seven."

Seven days? I would have guessed two at most.

"I was asleep all that time?"

"You were healing."

Her words were so calm and matter-of-fact. It was as though she were telling me the tea was ready or the sun had set.

"Is that all?"

She moved closer and sat at the end of the bed, just beyond my feet. "There are many ways to help a body heal. Let's not dwell on that, though."

I sank back into the mountain of pillows she'd piled behind me and tried a new topic. "I would like to know about my friends. What happened to Marlie Carlisle and," I swallowed hard, "Lucas Starwyck. They were taken. I don't know where. I'm afraid they've been hurt."

Mrs. Bellington nodded. "They're alive. Of that, we're certain."

I leaned forward, eager to hear more. "How do you know? Who told you?"

"My daughters tell me."

"Clara and Ada?" I asked.

She nodded.

But how did they know? They hadn't been with us. Or had they? Were they among the conspirators?

"No, goodness no," Mrs. Bellington admonished. "We've pieced bits together, the three of us. We can do that better than most."

Yes, of course. I remembered what I'd read in the records. "You were a Scryer, before you left."

"Retired. I left so the title could pass to Ada." She gave me a long look, and I could feel her searching my thoughts. Then she nodded. "I've continued to keep an eye on things, however."

The way she spoke made me wonder. "Were you watching for something in particular?"

She glanced out the window and stared at the hills beyond. "You could say that. I was looking for proof, I suppose. I've felt something wasn't right for some time. I thought perhaps it might show itself in my absence. I told people I was going to Yorkshire, but I've remained here, in the little getaway cottage my husband built when the girls were young. I suppose I thought anyone up to no good might become complacent after I was gone, thinking a young Scryer such as Ada could be more easily deceived. I understand you saw the gathering?"

How could she know? But then it came to me. My own thoughts had betrayed me.

"Betrayed is such a harsh word."

I closed my eyes, and my frustration grew. Was there no defense against this woman? Then another frustration took hold and quickly turned to anger. "If you knew what they were up to, why didn't you stop it?"

"I had no proof, and accusations like that without proof are very dangerous things."

She was right, unfortunately. Without proof, it was only one outlandish accusation against centuries of tradition.

"How many did you see?" she asked.

The image of them in the underground cavern came back to me. That horrible ceremony. "Ten, maybe more. And Mr. Bailey from Windsor Castle has been hiding there. He's helping—"

She put her finger to my lips and shook her head. "Do not say the name. Don't ever say his name aloud. The house is warded against him, but speaking those syllables will undo it. He could hear, and he could find us. Within these walls, he is the Betrayer, for that's what he's done to the Lady and the Fayte Order."

And me. He had betrayed me. But for that, I had no one to blame but myself. I should have known better. "Mr. Bailey and the other conspirators have dedicated themselves to him. My friends and I interrupted the ceremony. I don't know what happened after I escaped."

"How did you know where they were?"

Just as I wasn't sure I could trust her, I realized she didn't trust me, either. I could see it in the way she scrutinized my words.

"I overheard two of them taking food to Mr. Bailey in a secret room. It was very late, and they didn't know I was nearby."

"Seems an odd place to be at such an hour. Why were you there?"

"I was searching the old records. I had permission."

The glare on her face told me she still had doubts. She stared at me, and I could feel her combing through my thoughts again. Would she say something of my mother now? It was all there, laid out bare.

After a long moment, her cheeks twitched. Then, whatever inner debate she'd had with herself ceased. "Yes, I suppose that's true. You are new to our little community, after all."

Was that all she had to say? If Madeleine Ross were my mother, her sister would surely have more to say to me than this. Had Krol tricked me after all?

"Did you hear anything they said?"

I glanced up at her. "Who said?"

"The men. We're talking about the men, aren't we?" She was losing her patience.

I shook off my self-pity. None of it mattered now. He was the Betrayer. He would always be the Betrayer. "They spoke of taking meals down to the visitor and cleaning up after him."

"Is he a prisoner?"

"Was. The man was killed by…" I swallowed. "He had been there willingly, though."

"When you went back with your friends," she asked, unfazed by the news of Bailey's demise, "did you recognize any of the others?"

"Not at first, but I made the mistake of asking James Starwyck for help. We didn't know…" I couldn't finish.

The whole debacle flashed before my eyes again. How stupid I was! We'd made it so easy for him.

"He's one of them as well?" There seemed to be genuine surprise in her voice. Perhaps I wasn't the only one who had trusted him.

When I nodded, she went to the window where the bird had been and gazed out at the trees and the sky.

"I'd feared that was the case. I didn't want to believe it, but I feared it."

What could I say? I didn't know, so I let the silence hang between us. Outside the birds chirped, and the tree branches swayed. I could hear the breeze and the occasional pop and crackle of the forest.

After a long moment, I returned to the only thing that still mattered. "Is there anything else you can tell me about my friends?"

She looked back as though she'd forgotten about me. "Not much. They're alive, but we don't know where they are. That will take a bit more work."

"What kind of work?"

"Hard to say. We'll have to see when Clara and Ada get here."

They were coming here? "Is that safe?"

"As long as the wards are in place."

Her gaze moved to my legs. "Your ankle was broken, but it's healing nicely. It should be able to support your weight soon, perhaps another week or two."

I couldn't wait that long. "I have to get back now. Marlie and Lucas need my help."

She gave me a sideways look. "You can't go back to Balmoral. They're searching for you."

That may be, but I was the reason my friends were in danger. Nothing else mattered anymore. I raked my fingers through my hair, and finding so many tangles, gave up and pushed it back from my face. "They need me."

Mrs. Bellington moved to the hearth and picked up an

iron poker. She jabbed at the smoldering logs and stirred up a swirl of flickering sparks. "I know, dear," she said sadly. "We'll think of something."

CHAPTER NINETEEN

TWO DAYS PASSED, and most of the time I slept. I was comfortable, even if it was a far cry from recuperating in a chamber in Windsor Castle's Private Apartments. Usually, I sat and talked with Mrs. Bellington as she went about her day: cooking, cleaning, and gathering comfrey for the poultices she applied three times a day to my swollen ankle and other herbs she steeped into a tea.

"For the pain," she'd say when I tried to refuse.

So I drank a good deal, whether I wanted it or not. At least her meals were good, and I found myself eating more than usual. Though limited to the hearth, her food was always hearty and satisfying. A dark, rich stew was our standard fare, but sometimes she surprised me with green beans boiled with a salty ham hock and potatoes or a mushy carrot soup flavored with rosemary, thyme, and sage. A particular favorite was her pan biscuits. They were small and thin and served with a dollop of lemon curd.

After so many days in bed, with eating as my main occupation, I wondered if my skirts would need adjusting when I finally got back on my feet.

Each day I tested the strength of my foot by sitting on

the bed's edge and putting as much weight on it as I could tolerate. By the second day, I could stand with a moderate degree of pain, but it lessened bit by bit every succeeding day. By the following week, I could hobble around the small house without assistance.

One day while Mrs. Bellington was out collecting berries and roots, I took the opportunity to explore the dwelling a bit more. I opened cupboards and pulled out drawers but found little of interest. A few bowls, plates, and mugs in the cupboards. Utensils in a drawer.

I crept toward the ladder. Was anything up there besides her bed? With several winces and a few grunts, I managed to work myself and my sore foot up, rung by rung, to Mrs. Bellington's loft. It was a simple sleeping space, taken up largely by a quilt-covered bed and a wooden chest. Beneath a tiny window looking out over the front door sat stacks of loose papers and tightly rolled scrolls atop a small writing table. I recognized those scrolls. They resembled the ones I'd seen Clara reading in the kitchen.

I lifted one and read the handwritten message:

Good to hear she is improving. The others are still held. Not clear where.

A chirp at the window caught my attention. My pigeon friend was pecking at the glass. Around her leg was a tiny leather strap holding a new tiny scroll. So, Mrs. Bellington was not as cut off from the castle as I'd thought.

I hooked my finger through the window's latch and pulled it open. The gray bird stood there, shifting back and forth on her tiny legs. As gently as I could, I relieved her of her burden and offered her a handful of seeds from a bowl on the table that I assumed were placed there for the purpose.

I unwound the scroll and read:

HM and the rest to arrive tomorrow. Still looking for others. Fear we haven't much time.

HM? Who or what was HM?

From the window, I saw Mrs. Bellington in the distance, pulling what looked like wild onions from a clearing among the trees and dropping them into a basket. She wouldn't be back for a while yet, so I took my time getting back down.

As I slipped back under my covers, I heard birds chattering then footsteps scraped along the path. I knew Mrs. Bellington's tread, and it wasn't hers.

Every inch of me tensed at the awareness that a stranger was on the doorstep.

I wanted to hide, but where? Up the ladder? I couldn't clear it in time. Under the bed? I doubted I'd fit.

More footsteps, then the knob turned slowly. I jumped from the mattress and pressed myself against the wall beside the door. I held my hands up in front of my face in case it swung around hard.

But it didn't. The intruder inched it open.

I grabbed a pan from the counter beside me and held it over my head.

If this person thought a secluded cottage looked like an easy mark, they'd learn what a grave mistake that was.

Another step. Another. I squeezed the pan handle so hard my fingers burned.

Then, the intruder came into view.

An ash brown braid was coiled into a bun over a familiar kitchen uniform.

"Clara?" The name squeaked out of me.

She whipped around, and her gray eyes brightened. Then she noticed the pan poised over my head and blanched.

I lowered it and returned it to the counter. "Sorry, I didn't know it was you."

She lifted a single eyebrow. "Mother said you might like some company."

I stepped from my hiding place, forgetting the

tenderness of my ankle for a moment. I nearly doubled over in pain.

Clara reached out to catch me if I fell, but I righted myself.

"How bad is it?" She bent to examine the wrapping when I sat. "This looks like Mother's handiwork."

"It's getting better. I couldn't stand at all at first. Honestly, I was afraid your mother might chop it off."

Clara glanced up at me. "That sounds like her. Always the pragmatist."

"The swelling started to go down a couple days ago, and she finally stopped eyeing the cleaver." I was only joking, but sometimes I did wonder.

"She means well."

"Tell me about Marlie and Lucas. Have you found them?"

She sat back on her heels and shook her head. "Everyone thinks you and Marlie returned to Windsor, and Lucas's father invented a story about sending him to Inverness for supplies."

"So, they're getting away with it? How can that be? There were so many people down there. There were *Fayte Guardians* there."

Her smile vanished. "I know. They've been very good at hiding their secret, as far as I can tell."

"How do you know who you can trust?"

"We don't. That's what makes it so difficult. And there's still no proof of anything. Those who are involved won't admit it, and they're spreading lies to cover their tracks. The Fayte Guardians have never dealt with anything like this before. We've never had traitors in our midst."

"The silver lining is we now *know* there are traitors among us."

Clara and I glanced over to find Mrs. Bellington standing in the open doorway.

"And why are you on the floor, Clara Bertrice? Get up. You're a Fayte Guardian not a mouse."

"Yes, ma'am." Clara rolled her eyes at me and worked herself off the floor. She took a seat at the table. "You were saying? About the traitors?"

Something between a grumble and a sigh issued from Mrs. Bellington as she made her way to the counter, where she picked up the pan I'd set down and returned it to its proper place. "I can sense it. There's definitely something wrong. The trees are blind to it. It's their wards, I suppose. Or that creeping disease. Where is Ada?"

Clara dropped her glance to the floor. "She couldn't come. Duties."

"What duties?" Mrs. Bellington demanded.

"You know how things get when the Queen is expected," her daughter answered.

"Expected? When?"

"Didn't you get my message?" Clara asked. "She's to arrive tomorrow."

I shoved the purloined note deeper into my skirt pocket.

"No, I received no message." The corners of her mouth tucked in. "That's troubling news. Whatever the conspirators are planning, I'm sure they'll want to be quick about it."

"Why do you think so?" I asked.

"They can't risk their plans being revealed at the next Converging," she said as though it should be obvious. "They've been careful to hide their dealings from the Lady so far, but at some point, their luck will run out."

"Must she wait for a ceremony? Couldn't she intervene at any time?"

Mrs. Bellington mulled the question. "Yes, I'm sure she could, but it's the way things have always been done. The Lady does as she pleases."

Not unlike a certain dragonfly, but I kept that thought

to myself.

"So, it can be done," I pressed. "It is possible?"

Mrs. Bellington's gaze hung on me. "If there's something you'd like to tell us, now would be a good time."

She was right. There was no reason to keep it secret, at least none that was more important than saving Lucas and Marlie and protecting the Queen. "I saw the Lady at Balmoral. She visited me about a week before everything happened."

Disbelief then anger passed over them both.

"She appeared to you, and you didn't tell anyone?" Clara wailed.

"I didn't know I should."

Mrs. Bellington's lips pursed, and her eyes narrowed. "Why did she come to you?"

"To ask me about… the Betrayer." I stopped then. I clouded my thoughts to conceal anything more about our connection.

"Ask you about the what?" Clara pressed.

Mrs. Bellington hushed her daughter with a hard look then turned back to me. "Why would she ask you?"

"She wanted to know if I'd encountered him." I lifted my hands and waved them, reminding them about my visions. "After what happened at Windsor, she thought he might have followed me here."

"What did you tell her?"

"I told her I hadn't seen him, and that was the truth before last night." Inwardly, I winced, regretting the lie. Again, I muddled my thoughts to hide the truth.

Clara's wide eyes told me she didn't understand what we were talking about. Apparently, her mother hadn't shared everything about what the Fayte Guardians had been doing in that underground room.

"Still, what makes you believe you can call on her?" Mrs. Bellington crossed her arms, impatient for an answer.

"It's just a feeling, I suppose." I didn't want to be more specific.

"I don't know who this other person is, but if it's possible for Jane to call upon the Lady, we must try," Clara blurted. She looked at both of us. "Shouldn't we?"

"Yes," Mrs. Bellington said, rubbing her finger along her jaw. "We should try."

I sat back and watched them. I didn't know what to say, so I said nothing. Maybe I'd already said too much.

They both turned to me, expectation written plain on their faces.

"You want me to do it now?" I asked.

"Can you?" Mrs. Bellington pressed.

"I don't know." And honestly, I didn't.

"Would you try?" Clara urged.

Would it hurt to try? I saw no reason why it would, so I rose and limped toward the door.

Mrs. Bellington lurched forward to stop me. "Where are you going?"

"Outside."

"The wards can't protect you out there. You must stay inside."

"But if the house is warded, as you say, how will she hear me?"

Mrs. Bellington frowned. "Yes, that does pose a problem. I suppose that settles it, then. We must find another way. We can't risk being discovered by *him*."

Clara sighed. "For goodness' sake, who are you referring to?"

"It doesn't matter," Mrs. Bellington said and clamped her lips shut.

Clara's eyes went wide with rage and confusion. She obviously wasn't used to being shut out by her mother that way. "If you won't tell me, there's no point in me being here. I should be getting back to the castle, anyway."

Mrs. Bellington's face twisted with anguish. Unlike me,

she didn't seem accustomed to keeping secrets from those close to her. "I'm sorry, dove. I wanted to protect you, but it seems we've had a visitor from the Lady's realm. He's not like her, however, not in the least."

"What do you mean? How is he different?"

Mrs. Bellington lips twitched as she struggled to form the explanation. "We believe he intends to destroy the Fayte Order."

The color drained from Clara's cheeks. "Was that what happened at Windsor?"

They both looked at me, waiting for an answer.

I nodded. "Edward Bailey created the conditions for... *him*... to possess the Queen, like the Lady can sometimes possess a Scryer. Only I don't think *he* ever intended to release her."

"I suppose we should assume that's still his plan," Mrs. Bellington said.

"I'm not so sure," I said. "The men I overheard, they mentioned something called a Slivering. Have you heard of it?"

Clara frowned, but Mrs. Bellington's eyes went wide. "Are you sure that was the word they used? Slivering?"

I nodded.

The older woman shook her head. "I haven't heard that word in a very long time. It's unlikely those men have any idea of its meaning."

I bit my lower lip. It wasn't my place to divulge Lucas's secret, but they had to know the truth. I had to tell them everything.

"I'm quite sure they do know," I said. "When we were down there, *he* told Lucas that his soul had been Slivered. That Mr. Starwyck had orchestrated it, whatever it was."

Mrs. Bellington sat back hard in her chair. Either in disbelief or horror, I didn't know.

"Mother, what is a Slivering? What does it mean?"

Mrs. Bellington shot up and paced the floor with her

hand over her mouth. Clara and I looked at each other, confused but neither of us daring to utter a peep.

When Clara's mother returned to her chair, she'd composed herself again. "What it means is that this fiend is more dangerous than I thought." She swung around to me then. "I'm going to ask you something, and it's important that you be completely honest."

I braced and noticed Clara did the same.

"When you encountered this creature at Windsor, did you ever phantom walk with him? Did he ever take you beyond our world?"

I froze. She seemed to already know. Had she seen it in my thoughts?

"It isn't a difficult question," the elder woman pressed. "A simple yes or no will do."

"I don't know what happened."

She narrowed her gaze. "Are you sure?"

I shifted, feeling her prying into my mind. Yes, that must be how she'd discovered it. I tried to muddle my thoughts, but then I stopped. Why fight it? She already knew, and perhaps that was for the best.

Nothing to fear, Jane.

Her words came to me silently, but I knew it was her.

We cannot do this without you. We need your help.

Still, despite all that had changed, my instincts told me to hide this secret. If I admitted it now, what would become of me? Mrs. Bellington would know everything.

If you do not help us, you will be helping him. Is that what you want?

That was the ultimate question, wasn't it? I could not walk the line between one side and the other any longer. I had to choose.

"He took me to a dream place, if that's what you mean."

The Gray Woods?

I nodded at Mrs. Bellington's silent question.

She nodded as though I was merely confirming what she already suspected.

"Was that the only time?"

I shook my head. "There were others." I ran through them in my mind: the flight into the forest during the Converging Ceremony, the walk through the walls, and even that first time, seeing the silvery specter of my arm separating from its physical form for only a moment when Marlie and I crossed Windsor's Quadrangle.

Mrs. Bellington's face registered confusion then surprise and finally, quizzically, a knowing smile.

"I know that smile, Mother," Clara said. "You have a plan, haven't you?"

"Perhaps, dove. Jane has given me an idea."

"Have I? How?" Honestly, I didn't even care. I was happy to have her attention focused on something besides my private thoughts.

"Since Jane has demonstrated a capacity for phantom walking, I believe we might use it to our advantage."

"How?" I asked, sensing trouble.

"Wasn't phantom walking banned because of its…" Clara stopped and looked like she would have stuffed those words back into her mouth if she could.

Mrs. Bellington clasped her hands in front of herself, gripping them tightly. "The practice has been discouraged because of its unpredictability. But so far, our efforts have been hampered by the conspirators' ability to hide in secret places. Places you and Ada cannot reach. A phantom walker, however, can move freely. That's how we'll find Marlie and Lucas, and that's how we'll reveal the conspirators' crimes." Mrs. Bellington turned to me. "I believe you will be able to handle yourself quite well with the proper training and a little extra protection."

My hand fluttered up to the Faytling resting beneath my blouse. "What kind of protection?"

"You see there? Your instincts are already serving you

well. Yes, I am referring to your Faytling. What has Mrs. Crossey told you of the stone's power?"

Not much now that I considered it. Clara's blank expression offered no help, either. "That it amplifies one's natural skill and protects the wearer." When she'd explained it to me, I hadn't fully understood how, and I realized I still didn't.

"Yes, exactly," Mrs. Bellington said. "There is more to it, however."

"Mother?"

I couldn't tell whether that was a question or a warning in Clara's voice.

Mrs. Bellington didn't seem to care one way or the other. She went to a drawer and pulled out a sheet of paper, an ink well, and a pen. She quickly scratched out a message and blew on the ink to set it before folding it into a tiny square. She handed it to Clara. "Give this to Ada and tell her she must bring these items tomorrow evening. I want both of you to come to the cottage after dusk."

Clara seemed to hesitate. "I'm not sure that will be possible, Mother. Not for Ada. She and the other upstairs maids will be busy attending to the royal family. Whatever you need, I'm sure I can manage it."

Something in the way Clara stared at the ground made me think there was more to it, but she looked so uncomfortable I knew I couldn't ask.

Mrs. Bellington placed her hand on her daughter's elbow and waited until she looked up. "Even if it's difficult, Ada must come with you. You must make her understand."

Clara nodded.

Mrs. Bellington opened her mouth as if to press her case, but she closed it again and pulled her daughter into an embrace. "You're a good girl, Clara," she said with her cheek pressed hard against Clara's head. "You've always been a good girl. I know I haven't told you that enough, but I am so very proud of you."

I pulled back toward the counter, suddenly feeling like an intruder on this tender moment. I stared at the counter and brushed away crumbs from the morning's biscuits.

"I know, Mother," Clara said, but she seemed as close to tears as I was.

They both cleared their throats and parted. Mrs. Bellington straightened and took a deep and resolute breath. "Be off with you, then, lass. You have a message to deliver, and Jane and I have work to do."

CHAPTER TWENTY

MRS. BELLINGTON WASN'T kidding. After Clara left, we ate what remained of the previous night's stew, and when she ordinarily would have sent me off to bed, she put a tea kettle on the fire instead.

"I'd like to see you phantom walk," she said, pulling two fresh teacups and the teapot from the cupboard.

The request surprised me. "I'm not sure I can."

I could see she wouldn't let me off so easily, though.

"Please try."

I closed my eyes and did as she asked. First, I imagined myself as a silvery outline. When I could hold that picture in my mind, I raised my arm and opened my eyes. My whole arm had moved, not just its shimmering shadow. "It doesn't seem to be working."

The kettle steamed, and Mrs. Bellington wrapped her hand in a dish towel and pulled it from the fire. "Give it time," she said and poured the boiling water into the teapot. "We've got all night."

I suppose she was trying to put me at ease, but it was having the opposite effect. It reminded me of the first time Mrs. Crossey had put random items in front of me and asked me to reveal information about the owner of each one. Although it was something I'd been doing to some degree for most of my life, those first attempts under her scrutiny produced nothing but raw nerves.

After two cups of tea and several more failed attempts, I was ready to give up.

"Don't give up," she said. "You're nearly there."

By now I was used to her reading my thoughts, but I wasn't sure I believed her. I didn't feel any closer to phantom walking than I had when I started.

"It will come," she said and poured me the last of the tea. "Perhaps when you trust me, it will come."

"I do trust you," I countered.

She gave me a sideways glance and half smiled. "Not quite yet, I think, and that's all right. We will need to work on trusting each other."

She didn't trust me? I sipped my tea and let that sink in. I wasn't sure how to respond, so instead of saying anything I held my teacup close and watched the fire consume the logs in the grate. We sat that way in silence for some time, until she sighed, gathered herself up, and wished me a good night.

I wished her the same and watched her disappear into the loft above.

~ ~ ~

The next day, I awoke to an empty house. At least I thought it was empty until I heard the ceiling groan under Mrs. Bellington's footsteps. Sunlight streamed through the windows, which meant it was usually the time the woman was out collecting vegetables and herbs.

I rose from bed and made noise while I donned my apron, so she'd know I was awake. Still, I heard nothing from her but the creak of a chair.

The night before, she'd set out a bowl of apples to

make apple sauce, so I picked up a paring knife and went to work peeling them and tossing them into a pot of water so they wouldn't brown. When I put the last one in the pot, I glanced at the ladder. Was she ever going to come down?

"Would you like some tea?" I called out at last. "I can put the kettle on before starting the apples."

There was no answer. Instead, I heard wooden legs scrape against the floor then footsteps. But they didn't come to the ladder. The ceiling groaned at the northern end of the house, where her window looked out over the forest.

The walls were so thin, I knew she could hear me. So why no answer? "Mrs. Bellington? Are you all right?"

Was that a sigh I heard?

"Jane, if you have a moment, could you come up here?"

A coil tightened around my chest. She'd never invited me up before, and the somber tone of her voice put me on edge.

"I'll be right there." I wiped my gloves on my apron before removing it and hooking it around the wooden back of the nearest chair. My hands shook so badly, even that simple task proved difficult.

I crawled up the rungs slowly. When I could see through the small opening, I saw her standing at the window, staring at something in the distance, or maybe at nothing at all.

"Is everything all right?" My voice trembled almost as badly as my hands.

She turned and the slant of sunlight across her face darkened the shadows beneath her eyes. Had she not slept?

"On my dresser, you'll find a wooden box. Would you open it, please?"

I went to the chest of drawers and found it, brushing

my fingertips across its smooth surface. It hadn't been there when I'd visited the room before. I would have remembered such a lovely piece.

"Yes, you may remove your gloves."

She answered the question I'd been too nervous to ask, and I didn't hesitate. I yanked off my right glove and trailed my fingertips over the grain. The wood was warm and inviting. Instantly, an image swirled of two young girls stuffing it full of dried leaves and dirt. Even at this tender age, I recognized Clara and Ada. Both all giggles and squeals, and it brought a smile to my face. I wish I could have known them then.

"It's the pages within that I think you'll want to see," Mrs. Bellington said.

Reluctantly, I pushed aside the childhood image of the Bellington girls, lifted the latch, and gazed upon the sheets of paper resting within. So many pages and not all the same size or appearance. But all, every one, had a ragged, torn edge. I recognized the top sheet as similar to the pages of the ledgers I'd seen among the old Fayte records. "Are these—"

"Yes. They are from the Library."

The first handwritten entry was for Lavinia Ross's marriage to Henry Bellington and a note that future entries would be filed under Bellington. I scanned down the column, past retirements and a death of another Ross, and then I found January 1839. Madeleine Ross inducted as Apprentice Scryer at Buckingham Palace. I touched the black ink, hoping for a vision from the author or an image of Madeleine.

Nothing.

I flipped to the next page and found additional entries. Scanning down, I landed on her name again, this time beside the date June 1839. Madeleine Ross, departure. Reason unknown.

"Why do you have these?"

She'd been watching me. "I took them."

"But why?"

"To protect her, and to protect you."

I didn't know what to say. I was too afraid to say what I was thinking, but I hoped she'd see the question in my mind.

Instead, she turned back to the window and nodded.

It was the answer to my unspoken question.

She was telling me it was true. All of it. Madeleine was my mother.

I wanted to be angry. How could she keep this from me? And why tell me now? But the anger wouldn't come. What I felt was an immense relief. Finally, an answer I could believe without question. Finally, the truth. I stared at the pages beneath my fingers. "Is this everything?"

"Yes."

My heart thumped in my chest. Everything I'd been searching for, the very reason I'd come to Balmoral, was right here beneath my fingertips.

"Then he was right all along. He told me the truth about my mother."

Her chest rose and fell in a deep and slow rhythm. There were words inside her that wanted to be released, but she held them back.

"Why are you sharing this now?"

Her shoulders slumped. "You deserve to know. I've wanted to tell you for so long about my sister."

That word hung in the air between us: sister.

The implication was not only that I'd found my mother, but I'd found an aunt. I'd found cousins.

I had a family.

Joy and relief poured through me, but there was confusion, too, and disappointment. "Why did you hide this from me?"

She closed her eyes, and the creases around her lips deepened. "That is a more difficult question to answer."

She moved away from the window and sat at the edge of her bed. With her hands clasped atop her knees, she looked lost, almost scared. "Madeleine was such a sweet girl, and she had such spirit, so brave and independent. When we learned she had a gift for Scrying, no one was surprised. Everyone knew she was special. She had a remarkable way about her. So kind and thoughtful but also adventurous. She always loved her adventures. And such a beauty. You take after her in so many ways. I can see her in your eyes and the short, sweet slope of your nose."

I touched my nose and thought of the young woman in my visions.

"Unfortunately," Mrs. Bellington continued, "my sister could also be impatient and reckless. When she learned she could Scry, she was eager to use it and not as careful as she should have been. She would go off alone to practice, even when she was told it wasn't safe. The Council warned Scryers to practice only at the divining pool inside a Sanctum. My sister did not heed that warning."

There was a long silence then, and I knew Mrs. Bellington was swimming through old memories. I sat quietly until she continued.

"Madeleine didn't see the harm," she said at last, "and she believed the rule was unnecessary. So that's how she made herself vulnerable to that monster."

Her words broke off, and she fell silent as she fought back her emotions. I knew this was difficult for her, but I couldn't resist venturing the question that had vexed me for so long.

"Did you ever see him?"

She shook her head. "I saw the change in her, and I suspected something was happening. I assumed it was a young man from the Fayte. She always had so many admirers. It wasn't until she came to me in tears, after it had been going on for some time and it was too late, only then did she tell me everything."

"Everything?"

She slouched again. "That he'd abandoned her, and that she was carrying a child."

I knew this was the truth, but it still ached to hear it aloud. "So, he knew about the baby? About me?"

She shook her head. "Thankfully, no. And that's how Madeleine wanted it. She feared what would happen if he learned about you. She'd loved him, of course, but near the end, she realized there was something dark in him. When he left her, she said it was for the best. By then, she only cared for you and your safety. You must understand, unwed mothers have a difficult time, even within the Fayte. Perhaps especially within the Fayte. She could have endured it, I'm sure, but she didn't want you to grow up with that shame. So, she ran away early in her pregnancy, before her condition was known. I didn't see her again for years. When she returned…" She stopped and touched her fist to her lips. Her chest shuddered.

These were the times I hated my visions most of all. I couldn't touch her shoulder or pat her back or do any of the things people did to offer comfort or show they cared. A lifetime of avoiding the touch of others kept me from doing anything. Even with gloves, the fear of unwelcome images made me hesitate.

So much had changed these past few months, but this was still the same.

Or was it?

Would those images be unwelcome?

When she saw me reach out a bare hand, she pulled back.

"What are you doing?" she asked, not in an angry way. Just confused.

Honestly, I wasn't sure what I was doing, not exactly. But the more I considered it, the more it felt right.

"May I hold your hand?"

Two deep creases formed between her eyes. "Are you

doing what I think you're doing?"

I braced myself. "Yes, I think it might be easier this way."

She pulled her hand back, and I thought she'd refuse, but then she extended it, slowly. "Yes, of course. I have been hiding too much from you, but no more. You may see any of my memories you wish to see. You should see it all for yourself."

I set my glove on the bench beside me, took the hand she offered, and waited for the vision.

~ ~ ~

Images flickered through me. First of Madeleine as a child and then of her growing into a young woman. The sparkling eyes, the porcelain skin, the thick and wild dark hair. It was, beyond a doubt, the same woman I'd been seeing in the other visions.

This vision blurred again, and when it resolved, I was staring at the rough planks of a familiar kitchen table. The same table downstairs, in the middle of Mrs. Bellington's cottage.

Had something gone wrong?

An overwhelming smell of simmering apples hit me. But I'd left the pot on the table. It wasn't even on the fire yet. I turned to search for her and ask how that could be when I realized I couldn't. My body wouldn't obey the command.

That's when I realized it wasn't my body. This was another vision, and one so startlingly real I hadn't noticed it. I focused on my hands: They were scrubbing glass jars in a tub of soapy water. I searched around for more clues when a soft knock landed on the door.

Before I could even dry my hands, the visitor rapped again.

"Lavinia, are you in there? It's me. Please hurry."

The voice made my heart lurch. It was Madeleine.

When I opened the door, she rushed inside, wearing a gray traveling dress of the sort middle-class maids wore. No frills or fancy trim, but clean and presentable, and there was a thick knot of dark hair tucked beneath her straw boater hat. Tired shadows rimmed her steel blue eyes, and the lines around her mouth were deeper than I remembered from her encounters with Krol, but the wide, warm smile was exactly the same, validating the visions Krol had shown me and my own dreams.

All that fell away, however, as I—no, Mrs. Bellington—embraced Madeleine and tears streamed from both of us.

"Maddie, my dear Maddie, you've come home!"

My mother pulled away and wiped her fingers across her cheeks. "I hoped you'd be here. I asked in the village, and they said you often are."

"Don't be silly! You could have asked for me at the castle. They always know where I am."

"That's just the thing," Madeleine said, pulling away. "I can't go to the castle. Not yet. I needed to speak to you first."

The initial rush of excitement faded, and the reality of what Madeleine's reappearance meant sank in.

"Yes, I suppose you would want to avoid that place. But come in! Henry and the girls are out. Oh, Maddie, I've been so worried about you. Tell me everything."

While Madeleine removed her hat and cloak and hung them from the pegs by the door, Mrs. Bellington put a kettle over the fire and removed the washing tubs from the table to make room for a teapot and cups.

"I suppose you're wondering why I've come," Madeleine said, taking the seat at the table that was closest to the fire. She fidgeted with a fold in her skirt as though she wasn't sure how to proceed.

Mrs. Bellington stood at the teapot and considered her sister. Something weighed on her younger sibling. "I'm happy to see you no matter what the reason."

Madeleine's face fell to her open hands and she nearly gave in to new tears. "I shouldn't have stayed away so long. I've missed you, Lavinia."

Mrs. Bellington lowered herself at Madeleine's knee to look her sister in the eye. "You're here now, dove. Tell me what you need."

After another embrace, Madeleine cleared her throat. "You always could see right through me. You see more than anyone. That's why I've come to you first. I need your guidance, dear sister. I'm going to ask you a question, and I need you to tell me the truth. I fear my daughter's life may depend on it."

At that, Mrs. Bellington pulled up a chair and took her sister's hand. "First, tell me where you've been. I've been so worried."

Over the course of two pots of tea, they talked of the years they'd been separated. Madeleine explained she'd been living in a small village along the coast where people believed she was a widow. She told her sister she'd created a good life for herself and her daughter.

Mrs. Bellington sighed at the news that her niece had lived. When Madeleine had appeared with no child, she'd assumed the worst. But Madeleine quickly allayed those fears.

It seemed I was the reason for this visit. My powers were manifesting, and my mother feared that could put me at risk. She feared it could draw *his* attention. She never said the name, perhaps knowing more than anyone how dangerous it could be.

"Where is she, then, your daughter?" Mrs. Bellington asked.

Madeleine told her she preferred not to say, but that I was being looked after by someone who could be trusted, someone who would know what I was.

"I couldn't bring her until I knew the Guardians would

accept her. I need to speak to them first. That's why I need your help. If they know how powerful she is, do you think they will protect her?"

"Protect her from what?" Mrs. Bellington asked, confused.

Back then, Mrs. Bellington had no understanding of the threat Krol posed. But she knew it now, and I knew all too well.

Then the vision faded, and I was back in the loft, sitting across from an older Mrs. Bellington, my mother once again lost to the past.

"So now you know. Your mother loved you, and she was trying to protect you. She stayed with me that night and set off the next day to speak to the Elders. I expected to have her back with news that she'd be returning and that you'd both be welcomed back—I couldn't fathom any other possibility—but she never returned. When I inquired, they told me she'd never come to Balmoral. I wondered if she got cold feet and fled again. But that wasn't like Madeleine, not when she set her mind to something.

"I convinced myself I'd imagined the whole visit. I wondered if my grief over her loss had gotten the better of me, at least until I heard that a remarkable young maid, an orphan who would be the age of Maddie's child, had joined the staff at Windsor. When Mrs. Crossey told me you'd come to them from Chadwick Hollow, that's when I knew. Madeleine and I both knew Ida, and I knew Maddie would have trusted her."

"Is that when you took the pages from the Library?"

"No, I had already done that. I didn't think anyone would ever search for them. Our mother and father died long ago, and we had no one else. I thought I was protecting my sister from a legacy of shame. I wanted her to be able to come back someday." She paused then said, "I don't know what she meant to do. I can't imagine she would abandon you."

"Do you think he killed her?"

The question didn't bring the look of surprise I expected.

She shook her head sadly. "I don't know, but I've never stopped seeking answers. I've never stopped thinking of her and of you. We're family."

The word comforted me, but it still felt like a coat that didn't fit.

Yet I was happy to know that Mrs. Bellington thought my mother had wanted me, that she'd been trying to keep me safe. I still had so many other questions, though. Why hadn't she come back? What happened to her? Had she changed her mind?

And he had said she endured. But where?

"I wish I knew," she said, answering what she could of my silent pleas. "It's why I've put this conversation off for so long. I wanted to have more to tell you. I've sent out inquiries, but I have no more information about your mother."

It was frustrating, but this was still more than anything he had given me. As happy as I was to know more about Madeleine, it left me melancholy, too. A part of me was still hoping, even now, that he wasn't my father.

"I'm grateful for your honesty," I told her. "I know more than I ever have. For now, that's enough."

CHAPTER TWENTY-ONE

TRAINING WAS NOT going well. After our talk, Mrs. Bellington and I retreated to our usual afternoon activities. She went out to tend her garden; I stayed in to practice phantom walking.

Despite more than two hours at it, I'd only managed to separate with extraordinary effort and even then, only for a few minutes before I was forced back into my physical body.

By the time the late afternoon shadows crept across the floor, I was too distracted by my weariness to separate at all.

"You're tired," Mrs. Bellington said when she returned and found me standing at the window instead of working. "It's understandable. I'm sure it isn't easy being cooped up like this. It won't be for much longer."

"It's not that." I was still staring into the forest surrounding us, watching for Clara and Ada. "I just don't see the point. What difference will it make how well I phantom walk if *he* can still see me?"

I knew I had no right to second guess her, but I failed to see the logic of her plan. Marlie and Lucas were in mortal danger because of me, and now that the Queen was at Balmoral, she was, too. "How will I be able to find where they're keeping my friends? He can stop me at any time."

Mrs. Bellington clucked her tongue. "Let's discuss it when the girls arrive. We'll all have our parts to play, and we should discuss it together. Now show me how it's coming along. Let's see how much progress you've made."

What progress? I'd hardly made any. Perhaps if I ignored her, she'd busy herself with something else. But no, she took a seat at the table, and I could feel her gaze on my back.

"Come on," she said. "Let's not waste time."

I wanted to say this whole exercise was a waste of time. Instead, I pushed back from the window, closed my eyes, and focused on my feet before working my way up to my knees and all the way to the top of my head. I imagined myself stepping out of my body as though it were a shell.

When I felt the tingle of separation, I opened my eyes to see my whole shimmering arm lifted in front of me. Before I could look up to see if Mrs. Bellington was seeing it, too, my shimmer retracted back into my physical self.

I dropped onto the bench beside the table and sighed. "See? It's no better than yesterday."

"It is, actually. Maybe you don't see it, but there is progress."

Before I could argue, we heard voices outside. Mrs. Bellington was up and pulling open the door by the time Clara and Ada rushed up the walk.

"Did anyone see you?" With one hand on the door, Mrs. Bellington gazed out at the trees, searching for signs of trouble.

"No one saw us." Clara took a chair and let her head fall back with exhaustion. Her chest heaved as she tried to catch her breath. "We went to the dead patch first then wandered for a bit, like you said."

Apparently satisfied that no one was following her daughters, Mrs. Bellington closed the door and grabbed the carpetbag from Ada's hands. She opened it and eyed the contents. "Is it all here?"

"Of course," Ada said quietly, a note of irritation in her voice. "Do you know how many rules I had to break? What if I'd been caught?"

But Mrs. Bellington wasn't listening. She had the bag open on the table and she was groping inside. When she pulled out a familiar silver and gold vessel, a sunbeam glanced off it and made it sparkle.

My fingers flew to my lips. "That's Boudica's chalice!"

"You are correct." Mrs. Bellington positioned it in the center of the table and dug back into the bag. She pulled out the fist-sized crystal called Eithne's Stone and the Scryer Record.

I couldn't believe what I was seeing. I turned to Ada and Clara. "You took the Fayte Hall treasures?"

Both of them pointed at their mother.

She dropped the carpetbag onto an empty chair and stared at the hoard. "Not all of them. Just the ones we may need. They shouldn't have them, anyway."

"They?" I asked.

"The conspirators. You said they were using the chalice as a divining pool, didn't you?"

"Yes, but—"

"But nothing. They won't be able to hold a ceremony outside of the Sanctum if they don't have the First Guardian's cup, and now that the Queen and her family are in residence, we must take every precaution."

"Oh!" Clara straightened. "The royal family arrived on schedule, but they're only staying the night. They're leaving in the morning for a visit with the Camerons at Achnacarry."

Mrs. Bellington clasped her hands at her chest. "That's brilliant. When will they return? Did they say?"

"I was in the kitchen when the House Steward told Chef to expect them for Monday dinner." Clara's eyes shone with triumph. "That gives us—"

"Five days," Mrs. Bellington declared, then glanced down and tapped her fingertips, counting. "We have until Monday night, then. That's when they'll act."

"Why then? It could just as easily be Tuesday, couldn't it?" Ada seemed skeptical.

"It will be Monday. It's a lighter staff day. Absences won't be noticed. Trust me."

Clara nodded in agreement, but Ada looked away.

I was still trying to understand. "What is it, exactly, that you think we can do?"

Ada scoffed. I glanced back and caught her rolling her eyes.

"Did I say something to offend you?" I glared at her.

"You didn't have to say anything," she responded curtly.

"Ada!" Clara admonished. "She's trying to help."

"Is she? Or is she filling your ears with lies? Clara told me about the *thing* you say has infiltrated the Order. It seems awfully convenient, don't you think? That it's all happening just as you've come to Balmoral? Perhaps too convenient?"

"That's enough," Mrs. Bellington snapped. "Jane is our guest, and you will treat her with respect."

Ada folded her arms and shrugged. "Fine. But you should know the dead patch is still growing. Nearly fifty trees have died now."

Mrs. Bellington turned to Clara. "Is that true?"

Her younger daughter nodded.

"You think I'm responsible for that?" My voice cracked. "It's not me."

Mrs. Bellington held up her hand to stop me. "Ada, you know this began before Jane's arrival. We discussed it."

"Your theories. Your suspicions. Yes, we've discussed those. Shall we also discuss Jane's need to always be the center of attention?" She glowered at me, daring me to deny it.

Clara's face pinched. "You think Jane is making this up for attention? Honestly?" She rubbed her eyes, hard. "That's what this is about, isn't it? You're so used to being the center of attention, especially now that you're a Scryer. It's no wonder you can't stand it when someone else gets noticed or gets a bit of praise. You're jealous!"

"*You're* jealous," Ada slammed back. "You've always been jealous."

"Girls, girls!" Mrs. Bellington inserted herself between her squabbling daughters. "I will hear no more of this. If you want proof of what I'm saying, I will show you. Come here."

She went to the table, where she grabbed the Scryer Record and opened it. She flipped until she came to a page with a crude drawing of a creature. A beast, it seemed, but when I looked more closely, I could see what it truly was. The feral hair, the hulking shoulders, and that vengeful scowl. The sketch was rough but unmistakable.

"That's him," I said, dropping my finger to the page. "Who drew this?"

Mrs. Bellington stared at those hateful eyes. "Are you sure?"

I nodded, hardly believing that I was seeing him this way. "Who drew this?"

"A former Master Scryer. This creature came after her daughter, a young girl who was just beginning to learn the ways."

I recalled Mrs. Crossey's guilt and her confession to me after she was attacked at Windsor Castle. "Mrs. Crossey's mother wrote this."

"Mrs. Crossey from Windsor?" Clara asked.

I nodded.

Ada's finger was on the page, brushing along the handwritten script. She glanced at her mother. "You've read this? When?"

"As a girl. It was once an essential part of a young Scryer's education. The Council, or perhaps Mr. Starwyck, decided it was no longer needed, that the Order had outgrown the need for such things. The Unwelcome Visitor, as he was known in my time, had not been seen or heard from in so long, no one considered him a threat."

"No one but you," Ada said. This time her words held admiration instead of an accusation.

Her finger continued down the page. "It says, 'He calls forth his magic from a red stone worn upon his finger,' and that, like the Lady, his presence in this world requires a certain proximity to water.'"

"They need the divining pools, and the crystals in the First Guardian's cup make it possible to act as one as well. It was how Boudica Converged with the Lady during her campaigns."

"So, the conspirators can't Converge with him if they don't have it?" I asked.

"They will be forced to use the Sanctum, I expect," Mrs. Bellington added.

"That Scryer must have defeated him, if she lived to write the account," Clara said. "How did she do it?"

"Fire," Mrs. Bellington answered softly. "She attacked him with fire."

I envisioned a torch or a flaming catapult, but neither seemed likely.

Ada, eyes still on the page, began to read aloud, "'Every spell I hurled at him failed, so I turned one on myself. With cape, frock, and petticoats aflame, I threw myself against him. I struggled to remove his stone, but when that failed as well, I merely held him and after a time, he was no more."

"He died?" Clara asked.

"It doesn't say. She awoke in her bed days later badly burned. The end of her story says she dictated these words shortly before her passing sometime later."

"Is that your plan, Mother?" The usual pink in Ada's cheeks had drained away. "Do you expect us to set him or ourselves on fire?"

"No, dove, don't be silly. That way clearly didn't work as well as it should have. No, we'll need to get his Faytling. The Brightlanders are not invincible. They can be weakened in this world, just as the Lady was weakened when she lost hers. If we can remove it from him, I believe it will weaken him enough that we can destroy him. I don't see it around his neck, however. Jane, do you know where he keeps it?"

I'd never thought of it as a Faytling, but I knew of only one thing it could be. "He wears a red stone on his left forefinger."

"Aha, very good. We can use that." Mrs. Bellington said and squeezed herself into a seat at the table.

"Use it for what, Mother?" I could see Clara bracing for the answer. Fearing it, just as I did.

Mrs. Bellington smiled, but it didn't fool anyone in the room. She cleared her throat. "On Monday, after nightfall, Jane and I will enter Fayte Hall by way of the underground tunnel and search for Lucas Starwyck and her friend."

Ada leaned forward. "How? We have no idea where they are."

Mrs. Bellington shrugged. "It shouldn't be difficult for a phantom walker. The two of you will need to stick close to the kitchen," she continued. "If we find the captives, as I have no doubt we will, I'll free them while Jane fetches you."

"What if they have guards watching them?" Ada argued.

"We'll manage something, I'm sure." Mrs. Bellington winked at me.

What did that mean? I wanted to ask, but then I wasn't sure I wanted to know the answer.

"You two will need to be alert," Mrs. Bellington continued, "especially you, Ada. As a Scryer, you'll naturally be more sensitive."

Clara sank back in her chair. "Then why do you need me there?"

"We need you because we can trust you. We need as many loyal Fayte Guardians as possible if we're going to prevail over these conspirators. We cannot allow them to harm the Queen, and we'll need all the help we can get."

She straightened a bit. "You can count on me, Mother. I'll do it."

Ada demurred as well. "They aren't going to harm a single hair on her head if I can help it."

"Good girls. Now, you should probably get back to the castle. You'll need to be careful not to do anything that raises suspicion. If they think we're on to them, they may do something foolish."

The way she said "foolish" sounded more like "deadly," and it sent icicles down my spine.

At the door, Ada paused and looked back. "Mother, you know it's a completely batty plan, right?"

Clara and I froze and braced for another argument.

"I know," Mrs. Bellington said so quietly it was almost a whisper.

Ada cocked her head to the side. "But I trust you. If you say it'll work, I believe you."

Then she set off into the darkness. Clara followed after kissing her mother on the cheek and offering me a quick hug. "Be safe," she whispered in my ear.

When they were gone, I stretched, yawned, and made other ready-for-bed sounds.

"No time for that yet, dove," Mrs. Bellington said. "A bit more practice will do you good."

~ ~ ~

An unexpected calm filled me the next day as I made peace with Mrs. Bellington's plan. It was batty, just as Ada said, but it was doable. My phantom walking was improving, and all the practice finally seemed to be paying off. Separation was coming more readily, and I could maintain it for longer stretches every time. With a few more days of practice, I was sure I could accomplish what Mrs. Bellington was asking me to do.

What truly eased my mind, however, was knowing I wasn't going to face Krol alone. All three Bellingtons would be with me, and even though Ada didn't trust me, I knew I could count on her. We wanted the same thing: to save Marlie, Lucas, and the Queen and to stop the conspirators. Nothing else mattered.

If all went well, we'd also have help from Lucas and Marlie. The more I thought about it, the more confident I was that it could work, that it *would* work.

Perhaps I should have known better because all that calm and all that confidence shattered with the arrival of a pigeon at Mrs. Bellington's window that afternoon.

"What happened?" I asked. Clearly something troubled her. I could see the fear flashing in her eyes.

Instead of answering, she handed me the curled slip of paper she'd retrieved from the bird.

I pulled it open and read:

"Family left this morning, but HM stayed behind. Saying she's ill, but no one is allowed to see her. No one can confirm."

I read it twice. "Her Majesty?"

Mrs. Bellington nodded as she paced the floor, her heels striking in an angry, thumping rhythm. Her expression matched my own. The news couldn't be worse. I still wasn't ready, none of us were. But we had no choice.

If we didn't act now, the fight was already lost.

CHAPTER TWENTY-TWO

LOGIC URGED ME to be cautious and consider the situation carefully before reacting to Clara's warning, but fear for the Queen and the breadth of the conspirators' treachery was proving a far more powerful force.

And I wasn't alone.

By the time I finished reading the note, the usually calm Mrs. Bellington had yanked on a coat and was stuffing her pockets with bundles of dried herbs and roots, small jars and bottles pulled from her cabinet, and even Eithne's cobble-sized crystal, after wrapping it in a white linen handkerchief.

"Why are you taking that?" I asked, watching her plunge the priceless stone into her garment.

"Who knows what we'll need? Best to take it all." She grabbed the Scryer Record and seemed intent on shoving the hulking tome somewhere as well before giving up and setting it back on the table.

"We're going tonight?"

Her nod wasn't necessary. I knew the answer before I'd uttered the question.

Moments later, we were rushing through the woods

toward Balmoral. The sun dipped behind the hills, painting the forest in misty blues and grays. While parts of the path seemed familiar to me as we made our way along the hillside, I was thankful Mrs. Bellington knew the area well because I never could have found my way back to the tunnel.

Navigation, however, was not my primary concern.

"How will I find Ada and Clara?" I muttered when I finally mustered the courage.

"I sent the bird back to let the girls know we're on our way."

"But I haven't practiced enough. What if I can't hold the phantom form long enough to find Marlie and Lucas? What if I can't even get back to my body?"

She kept moving as though she hadn't heard me, but I knew she had. So, I waited as she moved ahead of me and pushed through a thick patch of bushes.

"We'll think of something," she said at last. "Somehow, we will find a way, and we'll manage."

I hoped that was true, and I thought again how grateful I was for this woman. For all the Bellington women, even Ada. I didn't want to let them down. They would be too generous to say it, but if this plan failed, the fault would be mine.

"Don't fret, dove," Mrs. Bellington whispered.

I'd been too wrapped up in my thoughts to notice she'd fallen back and was now walking beside me again. "I'm not," I said.

We both knew it was a lie.

"Just remember the plan."

When we reached the ravine, it was steeper than I'd remembered. I worked my way down slowly because the soil was still wet from the last rain.

"Do you need a hand?"

Mrs. Bellington was in front of me. She turned back to offer help, but as she did, I saw her left foot hit a slick patch and slide away from her. I watched in horror as she tried to lean back to stop her fall even as her leg kinked beneath her and she tumbled to the bottom.

I shrieked and rushed down to her. "Are you hurt?"

She rolled onto her back and stared up at me, her eyes wild. "Just my pride, I think. Here, give me a hand. I must have caught on a root."

Thank goodness, she was still her old self. I held out my hand and helped her stand.

As soon as she was up, her limbs buckled. She gasped and nearly went down a second time. "Oh, that won't do," she muttered.

I caught her elbow. "What is it?"

She took another step and winced hard. "It's my knee. It can't take the weight."

I moved beside her. "You can lean on me. I'll help you."

She ventured another step then stopped. "No. It's impossible."

Why was she being so obstinate? "You won't be able to get through the tunnel without help. Trust me."

She closed her eyes and sighed. "I do trust you, but I cannot go. You must go without me."

I heard the words, but it was as if she were speaking another language. They made no sense. I rubbed my forehead. "That's impossible. I can't go without you. This is your plan."

She patted my hand. "Take off your glove."

I pulled both hands to my chest. "No, we don't have time for that."

She reached out and took my hand again. "You must. I'll show you."

I yanked off a glove and let her hold my fingers. When the disorientation settled, I was sitting at the desk beside the window, writing out a message. Letters emerged and linked into words. "She's a remarkable Fayte Guardian. So powerful, yet she knows so little of how to use that power. We must help her learn what she is."

The vision faded then, and I was back in the darkness gathering at the bottom of a ravine, staring into Mrs. Bellington's wide, hopeful eyes. "Do you see?"

I nodded.

She tapped my hand gently and gave me back my glove, along with a bundle of dried, slender leaves. "This is sage. It can help to protect you. Keep it close, and it will hide you from the other world." She pulled out another bundle, shook her head and tossed it aside, then another. She touched her forehead. "There's a ward that might help: *Falaich mi! Cùm sàbhailte mi.* It's the old Gaelic," she added when I looked confused. "It means 'Hide me. Keep me safe.'"

She made me repeat it until I could say it just right.

"Good, good," she said finally. "Now, follow this path to the top of the slope. Go between those two oaks, follow the trees, until you see a steep hill covered in ivy. The passage is there, through the ivy. You will know it when you see the yew tree. Oh!" She stopped and thrust a hand deep into a pocket and pulled out a cloth-wrapped bundle. "Take this as well. It should help."

When she dropped it in my hand, the weight of it told me it wasn't one of the herb bundles. A corner of the kerchief fell away to reveal a shiny side of Eithne's Stone. "What am I supposed to do with it?"

I knew why she'd wanted Boudica's chalice and the Scryer Record, but she'd never explained what she intended for the stone. Did it possess a special magic? Was it like the Faytling hanging around my neck?

"I wish I could tell you," she whispered, her gaze riveted to the stone itself.

"This is no time for secrets," I protested.

She shook her head. "You misunderstand. I cannot tell you because I don't know. The trees told me to take it.

They didn't tell me why."

The trees. So, it probably wasn't going to do anything helpful at all. I shoved it in my pocket. "What will you do?"

She glanced at the ground, searching for something. Then she pointed. "That should be about the right size. Can you hand it to me?"

I picked up the thin broken branch lying a few feet from us and handed it to her.

With her free hand, she pulled out another herb bundle from her pocket. She shook out the herbs and wound the fabric around the rough branch. She took two steps, and it seemed to keep her steady. "This will do nicely. I can get myself back to the cottage. Don't worry about me." She paused then, and her lips tightened into thin straight lines. "But you. If you do not believe you can do this, we can find another way."

I trusted this woman, perhaps more than I've ever trusted anyone, but I knew she wasn't telling the truth. This was the only way. If I didn't get to that tunnel, we'd never find Marlie and Lucas and we'd never find the Queen. If I didn't get to them, Krol would win, and I couldn't let that happen.

I swallowed hard. "I won't let you down."

Before she could reply, I pulled out my Faytling, scaled the ravine's slope, and disappeared down the path.

I didn't look back, but behind me, I heard my aunt call out, "Good luck, dove."

~ ~ ~

I moved quickly along the path and repeated the protection spell silently to myself: *Falaich mi! Cùm sàbhailte mi.*

I didn't know if the words would do any good, but I needed all the help I could get.

Falaich mi! Cùm sàbhailte mi.
Falaich mi! Cùm sàbhailte mi.

The strange syllables also kept my mind too busy to worry about the plan falling apart and too busy to open my mind to Krol as I made my way through the trees and closer to my destination.

I couldn't let myself think about him or the Queen or Marlie or Lucas. One stray thought could give him advance warning of what we planned. He'd once instructed me to imagine myself in a ball of crimson light to hide my thoughts from Druansha. I had no idea if it would work, but I imagined myself in a ball of Druansha's lavender glow, hoping to hide myself from him. I squeezed Mrs. Bellington's sage sprigs and whispered her mysterious words:

Falaich mi! Cùm sàbhailte mi.
Falaich mi! Cùm sàbhailte mi.

My wounded ankle still ached, but it didn't slow me down through the dark and dank tunnel. I pressed on, hardly noticing the stifling air or the narrow passages. I pressed on, focusing on my Faytling and the words, and blocking out everything else until the tunnel widened, signaling I was close to Fayte Hall.

My heart quickened with anticipation and dread in equal measure. I could do this. I *would* do this. There was no question in my mind or heart. There was no other way to save my friends or the Queen.

The passage was wider now, and I knew I was close. But the air was still so hot and stagnant. I could hardly breathe. Maybe it was my frantic heartbeat. Maybe I wasn't remembering the passage as well as I'd thought.

Then, I saw it. But no, it wasn't possible. What had I done wrong? Panic surged within me, and I threw myself against the brick wall that now closed off the tunnel. I must have taken a wrong turn. There must have been something I missed.

There was only one way to know for sure. I tugged off a glove and brushed my bare fingertips over the bricks. They told me what I feared most. A vision showed me men laying the mortar and the bricks. The conspirators had done this. They had realized it was how I'd escaped and taken precautions so it wouldn't happen again.

I leaned against the solid surface and slid to the ground. Tears filled my eyes.

What was I going to do? I choked back a sob.

The image I'd seen in Mrs. Bellington's vision came back to me. *She's a remarkable Fayte Guardian. So powerful.* I scoffed. Not so powerful now.

I turned back and stared at the dark hole I'd traveled through. I could hurry back and return by land. Maybe I could make my way through the castle and down to Fayte Hall without being noticed. Maybe the plan could still work.

Maybe I was delusional.

I dropped my head in my hands and rubbed my temples, trying to think what Mrs. Bellington would have me do. What would Mrs. Crossey have me do?

Then I heard it. A small voice inside me whispered, *Walk through this wall.*

But that was a terrible idea. I couldn't leave my body stranded back here. I needed to fight beside the others. We'd already lost Mrs. Bellington. I couldn't let them lose me, too.

The tiny voice grew more insistent. What was the alternative? If I didn't alert Clara and Ada in time to stop the ceremony, the conspirators would win. Krol would win.

I had to do it.

Maybe it was a foolish plan, but it was the only chance we had.

I folded my legs and gripped my Faytling hard in my bare hand. When my mind calmed, I imagined a shimmering reflection of myself nestled inside of me. I felt it reach into my fingers and my toes. I felt it fill every part of me, and when I felt it completely, I rose and opened my eyes. The hand I held in front of me shimmered a ghostly blue. Behind me, my physical body remained sitting. And that's where it would have to remain until I returned.

CHAPTER TWENTY-THREE

THE FIRST TIME I phantom walked through a wall, it had been an accident, a startling and disorienting surprise that such a thing was even possible. This time, I knew what to expect. This time I was ready, or at least I hoped I was, for the strange tingling along my ghostly limbs and that unmistakable feeling of walking through syrup.

But there was no time to dwell on any of it. I had to move quickly as I braced for whatever was on the other side.

I needn't have worried. What greeted me was silence and darkness. No conspirators, no ceremony, and no Krol.

Good. I hoped it would give me time to search for Marlie and Lucas. I needed to find them and release them before the ceremony began. If I could accomplish that, we might have a chance to stop Krol's scheme.

But I had to find them first.

At least the darkness wouldn't slow me down. I knew my Faytling had its own phantom form, which made it tangible to me during my phantom walks, but when I asked it for its light, I discovered Eithne's Stone was the same. I pulled the brightly glowing rock from my skirt pocket and held it aloft as I set off to search the rooms and alcoves attached to the underground corridor.

My optimism ebbed with each empty room. I explored every nook and every cranny. I searched for hidden doors and even hatches in the floor. Where else could they be if not down here? Where else could Mr. Starwyck hide them?

As I made my way toward the staircase to check for other hidden spaces, I heard voices. Not a conversation, but something more formal, like an incantation.

I stopped. They couldn't have started already. It was too early; it would be too risky. There would be too many eyes in the kitchen, too many who would notice so much suspicious activity around the pantry.

But what else could it be? Carefully, I floated closer to the door. I extinguished the light of my Faytling and Eithne's Stone, then carefully—oh, so carefully—I passed through the door, just enough to see the other side.

What I saw terrified me. I would have thought the place was on fire, but the smoke filling the room wasn't smoke at all. It was a cloud of mist that obscured most of the floor. I searched for its source and found it pushing into the room through the brass vents. The machine softly chugged away, but instead of pulling the moisture away from the room, it was filling it far more forcefully than the divining pool ever had.

Standing in the great room, I counted at least a dozen Fayte Guardians in robes. They encircled one of the larger tables, which had been moved to the center of the room, between the three soaring pillars. Everything else had been pushed to the side.

What I saw on the table frightened me most. There, lying like a corpse just above the misty cloud, was the Queen, a small pillow tucked beneath her head and her charcoal-gray skirts draping over the table's side. The tips of her glossy black boots pointed to the ceiling above.

If there were breath in my lungs, I would have

screamed for I feared I was already too late.

Yet, there were only Fayte Guardians here. I couldn't feel Krol's presence. Under the light of the gas lamps, magnified and reflected by the mirrors scattered all around, I could see clearly enough, but every one of my more sensitive senses was consumed by the breath and heartbeats of the rogue Guardians hovering over her. When I finally felt the Queen's own breath and saw the rise and fall of her ample chest, my panic subsided.

She was alive, at least for now.

But what were they doing to her? I realized I'd never even asked Mrs. Bellington what a Slivering Ceremony would entail, and I cursed myself for it. Now, I had to wonder, did I have time to fetch Clara and Ada? Would their help come too late?

Fearing the worst, I held my place and listened to their murmurs.

"Tonight, we claim victory over the Lady who has betrayed us, who has led us down a false path for too long."

It was Mr. Starwyck. I knew his tenor, though I couldn't see his face beneath the hood he'd pulled low over his brow.

"When our new liege accepts these gifts, he will make us gods in this land."

Eager murmurs passed among those gathered.

"He asked us for the Queen, but we have so much more for him."

More? What did they do? I cleared the door and inched closer for a better view as a stifled yelp filled the room.

"You two, bind the girl."

The girl?

When two Guardians broke from their places, I could see what I hadn't before. Marlie and Lucas were here! Each was tied to a wooden chair positioned behind the Queen's head. Lucas's chin was on his chest as though he were unconscious, but Marlie's eyes flashed with rage, and she was struggling against her ropes.

At a side table, two Guardians stood over a metal bowl. One of them crumbled something dried and brittle into the silver vessel and another lowered the flame of a candle within it until a tendril of smoke appeared. He lifted it to Marlie's nose. When she tried to pull away, the other held the back of her head so she was forced to inhale the smoke. I could see her squirm, then her head dropped forward, as lifeless as Lucas.

My hopes crashed as reality set in. We were utterly helpless. The Queen, Marlie, Lucas, and me.

Do you see now? They are so weak. They will always disappoint you.

I was too upset to even be surprised by that vicious voice inside my head. I didn't know where he was, not exactly, but I could feel that he was close.

And I knew he knew everything.

Yes, I've known it all. But you had to see for yourself. I wanted you to see it.

He was so hateful. How had I ever listened to him?

Don't take pity on them. You are too strong for that. You should lead them; we shall lead them together.

Then he showed himself, emerging from a black shadow across the room. Had he been there all along, watching me? Testing me?

When the Fayte Guardians noticed him, they dropped to their knees, every one of them, including Mr. Starwyck.

"My liege, you honor us."

Krol moved through the room, and clouds of mist clung to him, only his black tunic and arms were visible above the billows that obscured his lower limbs. He gave Lucas and Marlie a brief glance as he passed and stopped to stare down upon the Queen.

Mr. Starwyck pushed back his hood and preened. "I have done all that you asked, Your Grace, and more."

Krol's granite chin lowered, acknowledging the fact but giving no sign of approval or anything else.

"Allow me to present additional gifts," Mr. Starwyck continued. He stepped between Marlie and Lucas and held out his arms as if he alone made the offering. "As I have proved, I can provide whatever you desire."

Krol's black lips turned up into something that might have been a smile if it weren't so wicked. I couldn't read his thoughts, but I knew enough to know Mr. Starwyck should beware.

My father gazed upon the man for a long moment before he spoke, and it took me some time to realize he was speaking aloud and not only in my mind. The bellowing, booming cadence remained the same. "Tell me, Guardian, do you do this for me or for yourself?"

"My liege! For you, of course. My only desire is to—"

But there would be no end to that sentence. Without warning and in a movement so fast it was only a blur, Krol reached out his hand and ragged red lightning rose along his forearm, shot from his fingertips, and struck the man's forehead. Several undulating tendrils converged into a single place between Mr. Starwyck's eyebrows.

I wanted to fly at Krol and make him stop, but I was formless and couldn't make myself seen to the other Guardians without effort. Only Krol could see me, but what good was that when he could so easily overpower me? So, I remained where I was, helpless.

Mr. Starwyck, too stunned or overpowered to move, stood paralyzed as a white light was drawn from him. Krol pulled the strand and formed it into a ball he held in his hand. When he was done, the shimmering sphere of white light hovering atop his palm was larger than a stockpot, and Mr. Starwyck sank to the ground. His bones pushed against gaunt skin, making him appear more skeleton than man.

I looked away in fear and disgust, and I wasn't the only

one. At least one rogue Guardian ran to a corner to retch.

Krol turned to those still gathered uneasily around the table.

"Not one of you came to his defense. That says much about him."

There were hushed murmurs. *Yes*, they seemed to be saying. *He didn't deserve our loyalty.*

Krol stalked the room, considering each hooded figure in turn.

"Or, does it speak to your own cowardice?"

The murmurs stopped. If I had breath myself, I would have held it. I could feel something sinister working within him.

"Is there any among you who deserves my trust?"

The hooded figures turned to one another, looking for validation or something else.

There was a low rumble of a chuckle. "No, I thought not. Not a single worthy one among you. Do you know what that means?"

One of the hooded figures closest to the tunnel broke from the ranks and ran toward the main door. He made it three strides before a red stream of light shot across the room and dropped him to the ground.

Every other Fayte Guardian froze and stared in horror, but once the defector was down, Krol raised both hands and took down every one of them. When not a single Guardian remained standing, that smiling sneer returned to his lips.

See, my daughter? They weren't worthy. None of them are worthy. Not like you.

I was too stunned to move or respond. I couldn't think, I *wouldn't* think, because if I did he'd know my only concern was for Marlie and Lucas, and if he knew that, they'd be dead in an instant.

Instead I focused everything on him. "What will you do next?" I asked, knowing he could read my thoughts.

What I was always going to do, and now you will be part of it. Come, stand beside me.

It was the last thing I wanted to do, but I couldn't refuse. All the dead disciples strewn about the floor was proof of that. I floated to his side, just out of reach as though that would make any difference if his intention was to harm me. But I put myself between him and my friends. I didn't know if I could protect them, but I had to try.

Watch me take her.

I did as he asked, standing completely frozen in my rage and panic, not knowing what to do or knowing if there was anything I could do. He lifted his hand over the Queen's face and splayed his fingers. I thought he meant to smother her, but instead that stream of red light emanated from his arm again, and he directed it to the middle of her forehead. Just like it had with Mr. Starwyck, it retracted after a moment and drew out a white stream of light. He was pulling the Queen's soul from her body.

As I watched, I wondered: Could he stop the process once it began? As soon as the thought emerged, I knew he'd sense it, so I had to act. I moved to my friends and placed my phantom hand on their Faytlings. I cried, "Wake up!"

Their faces flickered, giving me hope. When their eyelids fluttered, I wailed again. "Marlie! Lucas! It's me. Wake up!"

Something grabbed me from behind, and instead of that formidable stone-like arm swiping through me, it pulled me as though it had hold of my physical body and threw me across the room.

It took only a moment to register what had happened. Krol had stuffed the Queen's soul light into a silver bowl beside him and was stretching himself, and in that instant, I knew exactly what he meant to do. When he'd thrown me, that connection revealed his intention in a way I'd never experienced in my physical state. The awareness came whole and complete. I knew instantly he meant to gift the Queen's soul to his mother, but only after he possessed our sovereign's body, taken control of her throne, and turned her empire into his plaything.

It was a devious and terrifying plan, and I didn't know what to do. Then, as Lucas and Marlie emerged from their haze, it broke the spell. They were still in danger. We all were.

I still didn't have a plan, not really. I moved on pure instinct, and before I knew what was happening, I was pushing myself into the Queen's physical body as though I were returning to my own.

Once I could feel myself on the table, I matched my limbs to hers and stretched my neck. Wiggled my toes. It was beyond strange, feeling different flesh wrapped about me. I tried to move, and it didn't happen at first. But then I was able to open my eyes.

Krol was standing over me. His red serpent pupils glowered at me; his mouth twisted into a hateful sneer.

It was the best sight I could imagine, and I pulled the Queen's lips into a smile.

CHAPTER TWENTY-FOUR

WATCHING KROL'S CONFUSION transform into rage made my triumph even sweeter.

"Did you think I wasn't capable? That I wouldn't dare oppose you?" I rose from the table, straining under the unfamiliar weight of the Queen's limbs, and did my best to square myself to him.

You have made a grave error in judgment. You will regret this.

If he was threatening me, it meant I'd done something right. His anger emboldened me. "Have I, then? I doubt it."

Something crashed to the ground behind me, and I turned to see Lucas standing over his chair, now toppled to the ground. He stretched his arms, which were freed of the constraints.

"Help Marlie," I urged.

He dipped his head. "Yes, Your Majesty."

"I'm not… never mind. Do as I say. Help Marlie, then leave. Both of you."

Something near the Sanctum caught his attention. A violet mist was seeping from beneath the blue drape, pushing into the white mist still spreading through the main room.

When Krol saw it, he forgot me and went to the Sanctum. He pushed through the drapes, letting more of the violet mist billow in. Obviously, someone had been summoning at the divining pool. But who could have done it?

The question seemed irrelevant, though, the moment Druansha appeared, her pale white form standing in stark contrast to Krol's stony dark girth.

"Stop, Brother!" Her clear soprano voice filled the cavernous room.

He didn't stop. Instead he rushed toward her, seeming to lose all interest in me or anything else.

"Go," I urged Lucas again. "Both of you must leave. It isn't safe here."

Druansha stood firm as Krol neared her. "You won't win back your place in the Brightlands. Not like this, Krolaidh."

He sneered. "Perhaps. But I can still take this world."

"You don't want this world."

"You do, and taking it away from you will be satisfaction enough. I know you were the one behind my exile. To be fair, I also owe you thanks. If it weren't for you, I would not have found my daughter."

While they circled each other, I went to a chair. The body—the Queen's body—was growing heavier than I could bear, and I feared I'd collapse.

Near the door, I could see Marlie and Lucas watching me.

"Wait," I tried to say to them, but the words jumbled. It was all I could do to maneuver myself—the Queen—onto the cushions before her legs gave out.

Both Marlie and Lucas rushed to my side.

"Wait," I muttered again, and this time they understood me.

"How can I help, Your Majesty?" Marlie curtsied in

front of me.

I would have smiled if I'd had the strength.

"Get the bowl." The syllables tangled on my lips, so I said them again slowly. When Marlie finally understood, she grabbed the silver vessel containing the shimmering white light of the Queen's soul.

I closed my eyes and concentrated on me, on Jane. I felt my own fingers and my own toes, my own arms and my own legs. I inhaled deeply and lifted myself, feeling the Queen's body fall away. I rose and felt instantly lighter than air, as if I'd cast off twenty winter coats. When I opened my eyes, I could see the Queen slumped in the chair and my own silver-limned form standing in front of her. I touched Marlie's Faytling, hanging on the cord around her neck, then did the same to Lucas so they could see my spectral form. "Move the white light closer to her."

Marlie glanced at Lucas, and he nodded. Together, they lifted the bowl and set it in the Queen's lap. At once, her body straightened. Then, a point formed on the glowing sphere as if someone had pinched the edge and was pulling it toward the middle of the Queen's forehead. When it made contact, the whole mass of it rushed back into her corporeal form.

When the last of the light was still glowing above her brows, her eyes shot open. "What happened? Where am I?" She glanced around, confused by what she saw. "What is this place?"

Inside the Sanctum, something crashed to the ground and water flooded into the Hall. We gaped at each other—Marlie, Lucas, and I—but the Queen rose and marched toward the upheaval.

"Your Majesty, no!" I yelled and tried to stop her, but she couldn't hear or see me. When I realized it, I motioned frantically to Marlie and Lucas. "Get her back to the castle," I yelled at them. "She's not safe here."

Marlie ran to catch the Queen and was able to stop her

only when she blocked her path. "Pardon me, Your Majesty," Marlie said, her face a million shades of red. "Something awful has happened, and you really should come with me." She turned to Lucas, her eyes sending frantic pleas for help.

"Take her, Marlie," he said. "I'll catch up."

Catch up? He needed to go now. They had to get the Queen to safety. I wanted to shout at him, but he was already running toward the machine room's door.

How these stupid humans adore you.

I could hear Krol's words, but they weren't directed at me. He was speaking to Druansha, I could feel it. Something in the room ripped and snapped. Whatever anger I'd had for her melted against the fear of what he was doing to her. I'd been so angry with her for not telling me about my past, but none of that mattered now. I knew her. I knew her heart. I knew I had to help her if I could.

They dote on you like lost little children.

More ripping, more snapping.

What was happening in there? Torn between racing after Lucas and wanting to help Druansha, I left Lucas to his own devices and rushed into the Sanctum to find Krol and Druansha in a standoff. Her violet mist covered the floor and crept up the sides of the wall. Several tapestries had been ripped away and lay in heaps. What had they done here? Then I noticed a sleeve of Druansha's dress had been torn, leaving her porcelain-white shoulder exposed and smeared in dark red blood. A gash the length of a dagger. She staggered, dazed.

"What did you do to her?" Rage filled me as I flew at Krol. In my spectral form, he could see and hear me, but I didn't care. I only wanted to hurt him. I hurled myself as Lucas had in the underground room, and we tumbled against the wall as though I were in my physical body.

Only what she deserved. His words seethed through my mind as he struggled to push me away. *Move aside. This doesn't concern you.*

Glancing back, I could see Druansha hunched and limping. "Are you hurt?"

She glanced up and looked at us, but she was swaying on unsteady legs.

"Wait!" I peeled myself off Krol and flew to her. Her eyes fluttered and closed, then she sank to the ground.

She muttered something I couldn't hear.

I leaned closer. "What did you say?"

"The stone. Lavinia said you have the stone."

"Yes, but how do you—"

"She called to me with the chalice, told you needed help. Give me the stone."

I pulled it from my pocket, and she placed her slender palm upon it. Beneath her fingers, it glowed to blinding brightness, as did the Faytling around her own neck and the one around mine. When she pulled her hand away, the brightness receded.

"Keep it close," she whispered. "It will be your strength."

Then, with what looked like extreme effort, she turned and regarded Krol, who had yanked down a tapestry and was stamping it into the ground. "Go back to your Gray Woods, Brother. Go while you can."

He threw back his head and laughed a vile, menacing laugh. *How convenient that would be for you. But no, I think I will stay, Sister. I will erase your stain on this world.*

He grabbed another tapestry and pulled it from its frame.

She slumped slightly and whispered, "Jane."

I moved closer, ready to help if I could.

Her violet gaze found mine. "Can you forgive me about your mother?"

"Yes, of course. Yes!"

Krol paid no attention in his zeal to rip away the depictions of his sister.

A sadness pulled at Druansha's delicate features. "I wanted you to see for yourself. I gave you the spark of her light. That was my gift."

What gift? Then it occurred to me. "When you touched my forehead at my initiation?"

She nodded and winced from the pain it caused. "A clarity to your visions of her."

"You knew he showed me visions of her?"

"Not only him."

"The dreams? You did that?"

Say your goodbyes. They will be your last.

Krol had ripped away the last hanging and turned his attention back to us.

"Yes," she whispered. "The dreams. But there's more. Make him tell you what he's done."

I could feel him approaching behind me.

Druansha looked past me to him. "Is there nothing I can say to change your mind, Brother?"

His answer was a rumble of laughter that oozed out of him like a growl.

She bowed her head, accepting his answer, or perhaps just resigning herself to it. As the glow of her Faytling pulsed more brightly at her neck, she opened her hand, and I could see she held something. A small black ring with a gem that flashed red. I knew it at once. It was Krol's ring. His own Faytling, if Mrs. Bellington's assumption was correct.

Before he could see it, sparks of pink and lavender light shot from her Faytling and whirled around her, encasing her in its glow. Before my eyes, the woman shrank into the shape of a dragonfly and then, when the brightness became too much, I had to look away.

When I looked again, she was gone. I stared at the empty place then realized she wasn't the only thing missing. The thick, misty cloud had dissipated, too. The brass-plated vents along the perimeter were visible now, and they were sucking away what little remained.

Through the walls I could hear it. The low whir of Lucas's air apparatus. That's why he'd refused to leave. He'd ducked into that room to reset it to make it clear away the mist.

His subterfuge gave me an idea.

I could feel Krol again, stalking the perimeter of the Sanctum and watching me. I no longer feared him. It was a waiting game now. I only had to stall.

She's left you, just as I told you she would.

He was back to playing mind tricks. If Mrs. Bellington was right about what the loss of a Faytling could do to him, I knew what I had to do. "You won't succeed. The Queen is safe. They're all safe. You've failed."

He scowled at me then left the Sanctum. His stride was long and determined, but I sensed a stiffness that wasn't there before. It was already happening.

I followed but kept my distance.

When I emerged in the hall, I found the mist had vanished from there, too. He was stalking about, looking fierce, but I knew he was searching for the Queen. His nostrils flared, and his eyes shimmered with fresh rage.

Tell me where she is.

Good. He was more focused on Her Majesty than himself. I only had to keep him distracted. "It doesn't matter where she is. She's gone. She's safe. You can't harm her."

Another deep rumble of laughter came from him. *You think you can hide her? You hide nothing from me. We are the same, remember? You are my blood. You are my bone. Remember that. We can be together, the three of us.*

Three. He was toying with me.

The images I'd seen in my dreams, in my visions, came rushing back. I pushed them away but smiled as though I were contemplating his offer.

His lips turned up in a slow, stony grimace. *What did she*

tell you of your mother?

Should I pretend? But what difference would it make? I regarded him coolly. "That you abandoned her."

His head tilted with an unspoken question, but he remained silent. He stalked around me again like a predator. After a long moment, his response came. *I loved her.*

I scoffed. "Not nearly enough."

Perhaps.

Did I expect to see remorse? Sadness? I don't know, but he showed no emotion. How could I ever have thought I was like him? He only cared about himself. That's what truly made him a monster.

I will win. If you go against me, you will lose.

He believed those words. I could hear his conviction; I sensed it. He believed his words, and he expected me to believe them, too. If I wouldn't give my allegiance willingly, he intended to scare me into joining his side. The flash of rage in his red eyes told me he was done playing games.

What would he do when he realized I would never join him? Would he attack me as he'd attacked Druansha? I doubted I'd fare as well. But what could I do? I couldn't overpower him. My only hope was to wait, to hope time would make him vulnerable. I glided back toward the door and took my last shot.

"Where is my mother?" I demanded. "You told me she endures."

He hesitated then glared at me like he no longer knew me.

My sister tells you lies.

"Then tell me the truth."

Your mother is weak. Not worthy of your concern.

"If that's true, then show me."

He circled me, sneering. *There is hardly anything left of her. She is not what she once was.*

What had he done to her? Rage surged within me, but I had to ignore it for now. He would show me nothing more if we fought. "I don't believe you. If it were true, you would show me."

A deep growl rumbled through him. I was playing a dangerous game, taunting him this way.

I have no reason to hide the truth from you.

"Then let me near, so I may see for myself."

He growled again and seemed to consider it. When he nudged his chin, I took it as permission to approach. Slowly, I reached for his bicep, and at the instant I touched him, new images filled me.

~ ~ ~

Madeleine embraced his plan.

"Yes, Krolaidh, of course, I'll go with you," she'd said, her rose-petal lips so close to his. "I'll return tonight. We'll be together, you and I. Wait for me here."

She promised to return that evening with her bag, and they could go wherever he wanted, she'd said. She would follow him anywhere.

He'd been overwhelmed by her words and her kisses. It was more than he'd expected. Who could have known she would turn away from her life so easily? When she'd gazed at him with those deeply hopeful eyes, he wanted the future he saw there.

Perhaps if they'd left then, everything would have turned out differently, but he'd stayed by the stream waiting and gazing into the reflecting waters. That's where his mother found him.

"Bring her to me," she said.

Her visage rippled in the stream's surface. She had found him, which meant she already knew his plan. There was no use hiding or pretending.

He bowed his head. "Yes, Mother."

Even as he said the words, her threat repeated itself in his mind, reminding him what he stood to lose if he went against her.

He told himself he had no choice. When he'd left, just before midnight, he'd convinced himself Madeleine would be better off. They both would be.

He'd grabbed a farm girl on her way to a late-night tryst. She'd been only too happy to come to the aid of a handsome, well-dressed stranger. Mother had taken the Sliver from that whimpering fool graciously enough, too, and sent it off with her guard to wherever it was she sent such things, but when he'd turned to leave, eager to find a strong drink to dull the pain of what he'd done and the pain he knew Madeleine would feel when she realized he was gone, Mother stopped him.

She dismissed everyone in the throne room before speaking to him again. "You did not do as I asked, Krolaidh."

It was useless to play dumb. If she knew, it would only anger her. So, he said nothing.

"It's a Sliver. Does the source really matter so much?"

She stared at him so long he wondered if she were still weighing his punishment. Was there a chance for him still? But then she sat back, and he could see her mind was made up.

"It gives me no pleasure to do this," she said, "but I cannot allow this disloyalty to stand. If you want to be a snake, you shall be a snake."

Something roiled within him and doubled him over in pain. Slowly, the pain concentrated in his eyes. He rubbed at them so violently that he almost didn't hear his mother's heinous, mocking laughter.

"Go, see your reflection, my son. See what you have done to yourself."

His eyes burned. What had she done? He stumbled toward one of the rows of glass panels hanging on the wall, rubbing at his lids and trying to blink away the intensity of the sting. When he could finally see his face, he could hardly believe what stared back. His own magnificent dark eyes were gone, replaced by red reptilian horrors. "Mother, what have you done?"

But the question wasn't yet completed when a red mist engulfed him. When it dispersed, he was standing in the deepest, darkest part of the Gray Woods.

~ ~ ~

The images vanished, and I was instantly back in Fayte Hall, thrown several yards from Krol. He'd pushed me away and hard.

That's enough.

What was he hiding from me? There was more, I sensed it.

"What happened to my mother after you left her?"

He growled again and pivoted away, each movement slow and labored. Keeping him distracted was difficult, but it was working. I had to keep his mind on me, not his weakness.

"Did you see her again?"

I said enough!

His rage used to frighten me, but now I saw it for the opportunity it was.

I flew at him, not caring that he could bat me away like a fly. In my phantom form, he couldn't hurt me. And I could move so fast he couldn't react before I rested my shimmering hand on his arm and saw the truth for myself.

He had seen her. He'd gone back years later when he sensed her in this forest. It was a particularly wet and foggy day, and he'd come upon her walking among the trees beyond Mrs. Bellington's cottage. I recognized her dress. He'd found her the day she'd set off for the castle to speak with the Fayte Elders. When he saw her, I could feel the sadness and regret well up within him. But when he revealed himself, she'd screamed and run from him.

What she saw before her wasn't the handsome prince from another world, but a monster shriveled and marked by the Gray Woods with heinous reptilian eyes that flashed red and vicious.

At the sight of him, she released a single scream and fainted.

That was all I gathered before he pushed me off again.

"What did you do to her?" My mind spun. Had he hurt her? Whatever he'd done, she never made it to the castle and was never seen again.

That's enough!

He turned to come at me, but his movements were even slower now. Frustration fueled his anger, and he slammed his fist against a pillar as he passed it, leaving cracks that mimicked the marble's veining.

I let him nearly reach me before I darted toward the fireplace.

The Queen's soul would have pleased my mother, but you will please her equally well.

"I'm not going anywhere." I'd hoped to infuriate him, and it seemed to be working. He tried to spin around to grab me, but his legs moved like tree stumps. Every movement required strenuous effort, and the sneer on his face told me it wouldn't take much more.

He scowled at me, suspecting I was responsible but not knowing how.

For the first time, he was realizing I might have the upper hand.

His rage intensified. With whatever strength was left in him, he pressed up against the grandfather clock and toppled it. I tried to pull away, but I wasn't fast enough. The clock passed through me and crashed against the floor, the glass shattering into a thousand tiny shards.

You have betrayed me.

"You betrayed my mother. You betrayed me!"

Krol had somehow bridged the space, and his arm, the massive arm that had easily toppled that standing clock, swung at me, sending me flying across the room. I landed at the foot of the velvet curtain, a good twenty feet from where I'd started.

Your mother, that was unfortunate, but I had no choice.

"There's always a choice," I screamed at him. At least I

213

tried to scream, what passed my lips was something more like a groan. "You could have stayed with her."

You don't understand. You couldn't.

It was a circular argument, and what did it matter? There was only one thing that mattered. "What happened to her?"

Who cares? She's weak. There is still time for you to come with me.

I rolled off my side and sat up with incredible effort. I was growing weaker, too. "You're pathetic."

Am I?

He watched me, judging my reaction. He knew what I'd seen. How could he think I'd feel anything but disgust?

My lips curled into a snarl. "You're a monster."

You are a disappointment.

Fresh fire raged in his red, serpent eyes, and then somehow he was coming at me again.

The mist had completely retreated, and I could see everything clearly. At the sight of him coming at me, even slowly, I gave in to my panic. But I couldn't run away. I had to stand my ground.

Then, an idea struck, and I let myself fall backward. The curtain brushed over me. I didn't have a plan, not entirely. Part of me hoped Druansha might be there, waiting to fight the battle for me, but she wasn't. With the divining pool toppled over and dry, I didn't know if she'd ever come back, or if she even could.

Instead, I crouched against the wall and focused my breath. I had to do this. Just me. I listened for Krol in the other room. The instant I heard him get close, when I could hear his breathing around the corner, I launched myself and flew past him as fast as I could go.

"I'm over here," I taunted from the center of the room. He turned back, scowling and confused. "What's wrong? Getting tired?"

He growled and swiveled around. I could see it

required greater effort. How much longer could he last? With slow, but steady strides, he came at me again.

"Do you really think you can hurt me?" I honestly didn't know the answer, but I had to keep going. When he was within arm's reach, I laughed as loud and as hard as I could.

It enraged him, just as I'd hoped. He fumed and came at me, so distracted by his fury that he forgot his sluggishness and ignored whatever judgment he might have left.

I waited for him to raise his arm and for it to swing halfway at my head before I darted out of reach. The momentum of his movement couldn't be halted, however, and his powerful arm smashed into the weakened pillar, sending a burst of cracks along its length. The stiffening had to be getting to him for he seemed stuck in that position. I whirled around him.

"Having trouble?" I moved alongside him, close enough to see his eyes. He watched me, and the rage I saw there told me everything I needed to know.

His head stretched back in micro motions, and he released a bellowing roar.

Then it stopped. I watched his limbs and neck harden into absolute stone, his eyes dulled to lifelessness.

From above, a chunk of plaster crashed to the ground, and then another. Then the pillar snapped and tumbled to the ground. All around the walls cracked and moaned a death cry.

Balmoral's Fayte Hall was caving in on itself, and I thought of all the priceless treasures locked away in their glass cabinets. All the historic volumes stored in the archives above. I wanted to protect them all, but there wasn't time.

Something crashed to the ground with incredible force, sending up a cloud of dust and debris. When it cleared, I couldn't believe what I saw. A pillar had broken and now stood at a precarious angle. A portion of the top floor slanted down into the second. A cushioned chair from the upper floors had tumbled down and crashed through the railing, which was now swinging nearly loose over the center of the hall. As I watched, a second chair scraped across the floor, lurched over the edge, and tumbled down. I watched, horrified, as it hit Krol, toppling him to the ground and shattering him like a stone statue.

I stared in terror, but I had to move because the moaning, cracking, and keening above made it clear the place was coming down. The detritus couldn't harm me, but if I didn't get to my body fast, it would be buried here forever. I flew to the door and looked back only once from the hidden staircase. There were so many wonders in this room. The books, the scrolls, the artifacts. At least Mrs. Bellington had saved the chalice and the Scryer Record, and I still had Eithne's Stone. The rest would be lost. The soil rained in, filling the cavernous space and burying what was left of Boudica's belongings and Krol.

Flying through the secret tunnel, I found my body where I'd left it and wondered if anything in Fayte Hall would survive. In my heart, I feared the answer, even as I raced to safety.

CHAPTER TWENTY-FIVE

"**WOULD YOU PLEASE** slow down?" I was struggling to keep up with Marlie as she darted ahead of me. Her excitement was understandable. It was the first time she'd been given an order directly from the Queen, and she wanted to make a good impression.

I did, too, but my legs and head felt untethered, as though my phantom self still wasn't entirely bound to my body. I'd spent the night and most of the day trying to rest, but I was as wobbly and disoriented as I was when Marlie, Clara, and Ada found me in the tunnel. Thankfully, they'd helped me to my room and gotten me into bed.

I'd expected questions from Marlie. She'd heard Mr. Starwyck speak of my relation to Krol, but she never said a word and I was grateful. Instead, she and the Bellingtons offered nothing but kindness and care, and they made excuses where necessary to explain my absence from work.

That part wasn't difficult, considering I was one of more than a dozen members of the serving staff who hadn't shown up for duties. I at least had an advantage because my whereabouts were known.

To most people, the others had simply abandoned their

posts, which was making for a tense and frustrating day. It had worked in Marlie's favor, however, since her sudden reappearance was easily explained as a misunderstanding between kitchen supervisors. Her hastily concocted story about being called back to Windsor sounded reasonable enough, so she was put back to work attending the Queen's sitting room.

Since Lucas had also made himself scarce, it was left to Marlie to explain what had transpired to the Bellingtons, who in turn whispered the story to the Fayte Guardians who were left. They told me Mrs. Bellington was also doing her part from her cottage with her messenger pigeons.

Still, there was an unmistakable wariness in the air, and in the midst of it all, the Queen wanted to speak to me.

"You don't want to keep her waiting, do you?" Marlie had stopped before turning another corner and was looking back, waving at me to hurry. "I should have given you some of my golden root leaves. They would have helped."

"You know I hate that stuff. It's like gnawing on grass. Just let me catch my breath."

When Marlie finally stopped at a closed door, I knew it must be the one because she brought her hands to her chest, closed her eyes, and took a long, calming breath. When she was done, she glanced back at me. "Ready?"

"Are you?"

She stuck her tongue out at me playfully before turning the knob and parading in.

"Pardon me, Your Majesty," she said, dropping her gaze to the ground and offering a deep curtsy. "Miss Shackle is here, as you requested."

"Excellent. Send her in." The Queen's hearty voice always belied her smallness. Whatever the woman lacked in height, she more than made up for with presence. The slight up-tilt of her tiny porcelain nose, the squared shoulders, the hard-set jaw and stare. She possessed a regal countenance that made her the undisputed authority in any situation.

As Marlie stepped aside to let me pass, all the confidence I'd had up to that moment failed me. My knees nearly buckled as I crossed the threshold.

I found the Queen sitting alone on a white chintz couch. The afternoon light fell across her lap, which was hidden beneath a soft wool blanket, and around her were an assortment of oak tables laden with framed portraits, cabinets filled with books, and a mantelpiece mirror that reflected the bay window and the grand rolling Scottish hills beyond. Steam rose from a teapot on the low table in front of her, sitting beside a dish of dainty sandwiches.

"Please, my dear, take a seat," she instructed.

My wobbly legs were eager for the respite, so I settled into one of the wooden chairs pulled up to the table. "Thank you, Your Majesty." I kept my gaze averted as was expected of servants.

"Help yourself to the tea, if you like."

I reached for the pot and poured myself a cup. I wasn't thirsty, but the activity gave my hands something to do. Though the Queen and I had had a candid discussion at Windsor Castle after the Rubens Room ordeal, I hadn't seen or spoken to her since. I also had no idea how much she remembered from the previous day's events. How much would I have to explain?

"As you can see," she said, cutting into my thoughts, "I've already been enjoying the nibbles." She gestured to the gold-trimmed dish. "Cucumber and butter, with something extra, I think. Clara Bellington said she'd made them according to a new recipe you've devised. Is that true?"

I grabbed a sandwich and peeled away the top bread slice. Inside lay a few strands of basil chiffonade. I couldn't believe what I was seeing. "They are my sandwiches."

"They're what?"

My cheeks burned. "I mean, they aren't mine exactly, but Clara used my recipe. I'm surprised is all." Clara thought my sandwiches were good enough to serve the Queen? I didn't know whether to be happy or petrified. "You said 'enjoying the sandwiches.' Does that mean you like them?" I winced, knowing it broke every rule of royal etiquette to ask such a thing, but I couldn't help myself.

Luckily, the Queen seemed amused. "I do, actually. What's different? I can't put my finger on it."

She likes the sandwiches! If I'd had the energy, I might have run to the window and shouted it to the world. Instead, I sat with what must have been a silly-looking grin on my face. "Basil, ma'am. I only added a bit of basil and a few grains of salt to the cucumber and sweet butter."

"That's it: basil." She took another bite and nodded. "Wonderful."

Laughter bubbled up within me, and my hand flew to my lips to try to hold it back.

She must have misconstrued the gesture because she leaned forward, concerned. "What is it, dear? What vexes you?"

"Nothing, truly. I thought you'd brought me here to discuss... another matter, that's all. I mean, I'm delighted. Just surprised." I was rambling now. I clamped my mouth shut and forced myself to shut up.

The Queen set down the unfinished portion of her sandwich with heavy deliberation. Her smile narrowed to something more serious.

Oh no. What had I done?

"Yes, another matter, indeed." Her blue eyes flashed up at me. "You may be aware that I've been quite ill these past few days." She glanced over her shoulder, both ways, to be sure we were still alone in the room. "Yesterday was particularly fuzzy, but I feel I must share something with you. You see, I had a curious dream I cannot shake."

My fingers wound around the wooden arms of the chair, and I tightened my grip as she continued.

"I have a clear memory of being in bed with a fever and chills, and then things must have gotten worse because I fell into the most peculiar dream. May I share it with you?"

She waited until I nodded before she went on.

"I was in another place. No place I recognized but rather nice, perhaps a library in a country house. The strange thing is, I seem to recall being surrounded by a number of people wearing blue robes. But your friend was there as well. Miss Carlisle, is it?"

I nodded again.

"Right. Young Mr. Starwyck was with her, and someone or something else." Her slender eyebrows pulled together as she searched for words to describe Krol before shaking her head and giving up. "That's all very strange, of course, but I had the distinct impression that you were there as well."

"Me? Are you sure?"

"Like I said, it was a most peculiar dream. Have you ever experienced such a thing?"

The way she fixed me with her stare, I knew she was measuring every twitch and every breath. "That certainly sounds unsettling. Did anything else happen?"

Her head tilted. She was noting that I hadn't answered her question. "That's the thing, the dream faded, and the next thing I knew, I was waking up in my own bed."

"I can see why you would find that disconcerting," I muttered.

"Yes, quite. What do you think I should make of it?"

She was asking me? My fingers flew to my chest. "I wouldn't even begin to guess. But I suppose, since it was only a dream and no harm seems to have come of it, perhaps it's best to let it be."

"Let it be." She repeated the words slowly, stretching

out each syllable. "Yes, you're probably right. I suppose if there were any real danger, there are certain individuals who could be counted upon for assistance, are there not?"

I froze for a moment. Was she saying what I thought she was saying? Of course, she was. I nodded vigorously. "Yes, ma'am. Absolutely. You can be sure there are individuals who would do everything in their power to see no harm comes to you."

She sat back. "That does put my mind at ease. Dreams are silly things, aren't they? One never knows quite what to think of them." She bent down and picked up another sandwich. "These are a pure delight. Basil and salt, who would have thought? Tell me again, what do you do in the kitchen?"

"I'm a maid, Your Majesty."

"Yes, well, we shall have to do something about that."

~ ~ ~

When I descended the stone staircase to what used to be the tunnel's antechamber, I didn't need to remove my gloves to feel the sense of loss that still hung over the place. Until the rubble could be cleared, there was no way to reach Fayte Hall, so the Guardians—at least those of us who were left—were gathering in the antechamber to hold the Converging Ceremony.

Marlie was already there, talking in low tones with Clara and Ada.

"There you are."

I turned to find Lucas beside me, fastening a robe from a makeshift rack. He handed one to me.

"I wasn't sure you'd come," he added.

"I couldn't miss this. I think I need it, to be honest."

"You're not alone."

I grinned to appease him, but we both knew it wasn't genuine.

"That's a start, I guess."

"I'll work on it."

I saw Ivy walk by, and the two of them exchanged a hurried glance. The sight of it struck me like a dagger in the heart.

"I won't keep you," I said.

He glanced again at Ivy.

That was my cue to make a hasty retreat. I searched for Marlie in the crowd.

He took my arm. "Don't go." His voice was desperate.

"But won't Ivy…" I couldn't bring myself to finish the question.

"I know you'll be heading back to Windsor soon, but I wanted you to know the engagement is off."

I glanced at Ivy. She'd joined her friends and seemed blissfully unconcerned with us. "Since when?"

"We talked yesterday."

I hadn't left my room. Perhaps I should have. "She seems to be taking it well."

He scoffed. "She should. She's the one who broke it off."

"Oh."

"I was going to, but when we finally had a moment alone, she beat me to it. She said it was what her family thought best. How did she put it? 'So much has happened, and you need some time to grieve.' I suppose she was doing her best to be gracious because, while she didn't say it outright, I suspect there have been rumors about the events that transpired down here and my father's part in it. To be fair, I don't blame her for washing her hands of me. I certainly wasn't an ideal match. I'm sure she and her family were only interested in the advantage that would come from marrying the High Councilor's son, anyway. On my own merits, I'm no prize."

He was trying to have a sense of humor about it, but there was pain beneath the surface of his words. And why wouldn't there be? He'd endured so much. His whole life had been shadowed by the death of his mother and the disdain of his father, and then to learn the sorrow he'd been living with was something far more sinister. It was a betrayal few in this world could ever understand.

I didn't even know if I understood it, but my heart went out to him. "We'll have to agree to disagree on that point. Anyone with any sense at all knows you are very much a prize, Lucas Starwyck, so it's her loss. And if anyone should be held responsible for the actions of a father…"

He touched my elbow and shook his head. "None of it is your fault. You know that, don't you?"

I swallowed away that pain and pushed it from my thoughts. Now wasn't the time for it. "Do you know what you'll do? I mean, about… what happened?" It was a ridiculous way to describe having a part of your soul torn out of you, but I didn't know how else to put it.

"I'm still trying to understand it, but at least now I know the truth." Lucas lowered his voice so no one else could hear him. "I've always wondered why I felt the way I did. I just thought a part of me had died with my mother."

I nodded, but I didn't want to interrupt. Such emotion in him was rare.

"At first, it didn't feel like anything," he continued. "The pain of losing her was almost more than I could bear. I knew my father resented me, and I understood it. I didn't know how much he truly hated me, though. In time, I stopped wanting his love. I did my work and performed my Guardian duties. For a while, that was enough. When it wasn't any longer, I focused on being good at what I did. I immersed myself in building and maintaining this place and the air apparatus." He spread out his hands and looked around. "I took on as much as I could and told myself it was a healthy distraction. This was science, not the vagaries of magic. It was real.

"But I see now it was just another way I was trying to earn his approval. I didn't realize it was already too late. At least now I know the sadness I felt, all that emptiness, wasn't merely in my head. I wasn't imagining it. That's something, I suppose."

I wanted to comfort him, but I didn't know how. "Once a soul is Slivered," I said, "there must be a way to restore it."

"I don't know. Maybe there is. Any hope of learning how to do it, though, is buried somewhere under all that debris."

I didn't understand how he could take the news so lightly, but then that was the problem wasn't it? That missing part of him dulled his emotions. Love, anger, and everything in between.

"If there is a way, we will find it. I promise you."

He nodded, but I saw no fire in his eyes.

Someone chimed the bell to indicate it was time.

"Right now, I must focus on rebuilding. I don't know how we're going to do it. Honestly, I don't even know if it can be done. We've warded the area to keep others away, but it may not be enough. Which reminds me, the House Steward wanted to speak to me before the ceremony about his ideas on the cleanup effort. I hope I'll see you again before you leave, however."

He was lingering, and I thought there was more he wanted to say.

"Of course. I won't leave without saying goodbye."

Goodbye, had it really come to that? I wanted to pull back the word the instant it was out. I also wanted him to protest. I wanted him to tell me he didn't want us to part, that we should stay together, that somehow we could find a way.

He reached out to touch my hand, and he seemed on the verge of saying something, but he stopped himself and offered a half smile. "I hope that's a promise," he said and turned away.

That's when I knew: He felt something for me, too. I didn't know what, and maybe he didn't, either. But there was something there.

It made me smile as he strode off toward a group gathered on the other side of the tunnel.

"It's time, everyone," Ada said, kneeling in her violet robe beside Boudica's chalice, which sat on the ground in the middle of the circle as a substitute for the divining pool. She closed her eyes, dipped her fingers into the water, and recited the incantation to Converge with the Lady. Beside her, looking as regal as the Queen herself, stood Mrs. Bellington. She caught my eye and motioned for me to join her.

"I'm so pleased you're here," she whispered. "I was afraid you wouldn't make it."

"I couldn't miss this."

Ada paused to give us a disapproving look, then smiled and winked.

"Sorry," I mouthed as she continued the incantation.

Then mist billowed over the sides of the silver cup, obscuring the floor and our feet, a sign that not only the Lady's message, but Druansha herself would make an appearance. But instead of glowing as they usually did before a Lady's Convergence, the Faytlings that rested on every chest remained dull. Confused murmurs filled the room.

We could all feel it. Something wasn't right.

Ada cleared her throat and repeated the words more forcefully. Again, the strangely mixed response. The hooded figures turned back and forth, seeking an explanation.

Ada glanced up at her mother. "Have I done something wrong?"

Before Mrs. Bellington could answer, the mist swirled into a column above the chalice, an indication the Lady was present. The Fayte Guardians settled and waited in anxious anticipation.

A crackling sound emerged from the heart of the column then smoky tendrils of aquamarine stretched out and coiled about the center of it before pulling apart to create what looked like a gaping hole in the mist.

I stared as everyone did, waiting to see why the Lady would reveal herself this way.

We all waited, mesmerized, until something moved within the dark expanse. It was an alabaster staff, topped by a crystal orb pulsing in the same aquamarine hue. What appeared next was a slender, alabaster hand with long talon-like fingers and sharply tapered nails. Then a narrow, slippered foot stepped through.

When a head emerged, it was clear this was not Druansha, but someone else entirely.

Her sharply angled eyes stared at us from beneath thin gray eyebrows arched over a white porcelain forehead. Pale hair smoothed back from her teardrop ears and fell to the middle of her back.

It took only a moment to realize I knew this woman, if that's what she was. I knew her from my visions. She was the Brightlands Queen. Krol's tormentor and mother.

My grandmother, it would seem.

I stood as stunned and silent as the others, awed and unnerved by her presence.

Her icy gaze made its way entirely around the room before it landed on me. Then, and only then, did something flicker across her blank expression.

"You," she said, her voice haunting and determined. "You are the one who destroyed my son. Did you think I could let that stand?"

A flash of violet lightning flickered behind her in the portal, and Druansha appeared, frantic and breathless. "Mother, no! I beg you, do not do this."

The Queen turned to Druansha and offered only a hint

of surprise. "You expect me to do nothing? I will take the half-breed." Before Druansha could object and before I could move, the woman aimed the crystal end of her staff at me, and a stream of turquoise light struck the Faytling resting on my chest.

"No, Mother!" was the last thing I heard before the world faded to black.

When awareness returned, it crept back slowly. At first there was only an aching in my head, then an intense coldness against my cheek and the realization I was lying on the floor. But this wasn't the antechamber's floor or any floor I knew.

I cracked open my eyes to see these stones were milky white with tiny veins of shimmering blue. When I tilted my head, I could see I was in a cavernous room where every surface, every edge, exuded a softly iridescent glow.

Behind me, something pounded so hard I could feel the vibrations along the floor. With intense effort, I pushed myself up to see a great throne at the center of the room. Upon it sat the ghostly woman who had interrupted our Converging Ceremony. She scowled down at me.

"You're awake. Good. It's time you answer for your crimes against the Brightlands."

The End

—————

If you'd like to continue Jane's magical journey, the story continues in *Shadow Rite: The Queen's Fayte Book Three*. Learn more at www.DDCroix.com/Shadow-Rite.

DEAR READER

Thank you for taking time to read *Slivering Curse: The Queen's Fayte Book Two*. I had so much fun writing this adventure for my favorite Fayte Guardian and watching her take her first tentative steps away from being just an outcast maid whose best friend is a dragonfly to a more mature, but still insecure member of the royal servant ranks and the Fayte Guardian community. Like all of us, you can bet she'll keep growing in future adventures, and I hope you'll be part of that journey, too. If you enjoyed the story, please consider leaving a review at Amazon or Goodreads.com. Good reviews and positive word of mouth are immensely helpful and always deeply appreciated.

FREE BOOK

To get a free copy of *Memory Thief*, a prequel story about the events preceding Jane Shackle's arrival at Windsor Castle, and to be notified by email of new releases, join the Readers Brigade at www.DDCroix.com/readers-brigade.

ABOUT THE AUTHOR

D.D. Croix is an award-winning author who writes delightfully dark fantasy with hopeful and bright ever afters. Under another name, she also writes award-winning romance and historical novels. When she isn't plotting new adventures for her characters, she oversees Orange County Writers, a network of published and aspiring authors based in Southern California.

If you'd like to be notified of new releases and have access to exclusive content, giveaways, and other fun stuff, please join the Readers Brigade: www.DDCroix.com/Readers-Brigade.

If you'd like to send her a message, please contact her at dd@ddcroix.com.

To connect on social media, you can find her at the following:

Facebook: www.facebook.com/DDCroix
Twitter: www.twitter.com/DDCroixWrites
Instagram: www.instagram.com/DDCroixWrites
Pinterest: www.pinterest.com/DDCroixWrites
Goodreads: www.goodreads.com/user/show/77702468-d-d-croix

ACKNOWLEDGMENTS

Books take months, if not years, to write, so it's practically a given that the author will encounter unforeseen obstacles along the way. Sometimes it's good news that sends your life in an exciting new direction. Sometimes it's not, and you must deal with the challenges it brings.

Although I'm a bit of a control freak, I can usually take that uncertainty in stride and stay on track. But holy crackers, trying to write a book during a global pandemic has been… a lot.

Luckily, I had most of the story in my brain even if it wasn't yet on the page before our part of the world (probably yours, too) shut down. After that, all routines went out the window: the writing routine, the family routine, the school routine, everything.

At first, it was nearly impossible to sit at the keyboard and listen as Jane told me her story. It seemed like I had so many more important things to do: check in with friends and family, track down toilet paper and hand sanitizer, figure out which markets had milk and eggs in stock.

It wasn't long, though, before I was looking forward to working on the story again. As crazy as Jane's world got, it didn't seem nearly as crazy as my real world.

It also helped to know I wasn't alone. I'm deeply grateful for the members of O.C. Writers, who are never more than an email message or Facebook post away and can always be counted on for support and encouragement. I also truly appreciate the friends and fans who helped make *Dragonfly Maid* an Amazon bestseller (gaslamp fantasy category) earlier this year, especially Shannon Cramer, Gayle Carline, and Russell Nohelty.

Without Karri Klawiter, who created the amazing cover art and design, and Katrina Roets, who edited the manuscript, *Slivering Curse* wouldn't look nearly as good as she does, and I can't thank these talented ladies enough for their professional expertise.

Finally, I'd like to say this book never would have happened without the love and patience of my two favorite people on the planet: my husband, who kindly overlooks the late dinners and stacks of notebooks that accumulate wherever I take my computer, and my darling daughter, who tolerates a mommy who spends more time playing make-believe than she does. They are the true magic in my world.

www.ingramcontent.com/pod-product-compliance
Lightning Source LLC
Chambersburg PA
CBHW051239250626
47155CB00009B/3098